Cranberries & Criminals

A Paranormal Witch Cozy Mystery

Book Store Cozy Mystery Series
Book 9

Lucinda Race

MC Two Press

This book is a work of fiction. Names, characters, places, and incidents are the product of the author's imagination or are used fictitiously. Any resemblance to actual events, locales, or persons, living or dead, is coincidental.
Copyright © 2024 Lucinda Race

All rights reserved, including the right to reproduce, distribute, or transmit in any form or by any means. For information regarding subsidiary rights, please contact the Author Lucinda Race.

Editor Trish Long
Proof Reader NN Light Editing Services
Cover design by Mariah Sinclair

Manufactured in the United States of America
First Edition November 2024

Print Edition ISBN 978-1-954520-85-1
E-book ISBN 978-1-954520-84-4

1. Robin's Cafe
2. Bygone Antiques
3. The Pembroke Cliffs
4. Cozy Nook Bookstore
5. Twisted Scissors Hair Salon
6. Betty's Market
7. Old Town Library
8. Miss Judy's Dance Studio
9. The Sweet Spot Baker
10. Bee Bee's Boutique
11. Tuckers Hardware Store
12. The Copper Kettle
13. Police Station
14. Town Hall

Chapter 1
Lily

QUICK NOTE: If you enjoy Cranberries & Criminals, be sure to check out my offer for a FREE novella at the end. With that, happy reading.

* * *

I hurried through the town green taking the shortcut from my bookstore to my favorite bakery, the Sweet Spot. Well, the only one in my charming town of Pembroke Cove. The crisp air tingled my nose as I inhaled, pulling the cold November air deep into my lungs. Despite the sun climbing in the bright blue cloudless sky, I pulled the collar of my jacket closer to my chin. Waiting on the sidewalk outside the shop was my best friend and fellow witch, Nikki. I drew closer and she greeted me with a grin.

"Hey, Lily." She gave me a quick hug. "Thanks for getting me out of my kitchen. I've been rushing to finish my frozen pies that are on pre-order for Thanksgiving. I can't believe how many people want to bake off their pies so they'll be freshly baked this year, but it makes it easier for me."

Nikki was an amazing baker and supplied most of the restaurants up and down the coast with desserts as well as specialty products like wedding cakes and holiday pies. Me? On most days I had trouble boiling water. "I'm just glad you're up for coffee, and William has the magic touch when it comes to the cinnamon pecan buns that I can't get enough of."

She laughed and pulled open the heavy glass door. "That's the one thing I'll never even think of trying to make. No one could ever bake them like William."

I walked inside and, for a moment, closed my eyes, letting the smell of yeast, sugar, and cinnamon wrap around me like a cozy blanket while my mouth watered. The display case caught my eye. I audibly groaned and grabbed her arm. "Nikki, he has the buns but also chocolate croissants." I patted my midsection and thought of my fiancé Gage Erikson. We were close to setting a date for our wedding. If I added to my curves, who knew if I'd be able to wear my mom's dress.

She leaned over my shoulder. "I know what you're thinking. You'll look beautiful on that special day. I promise."

Giving her a playful swat, I asked, "How do you do that?"

"For as long as we've been best friends, how could we not know what the other is thinking on most days."

I flashed her a grin. "True." A paper pinned to the corkboard above the coffee urns caught my attention. "What's that?" Crossing the short distance, I read out loud, "Cranberry Bake-Off."

Nikki came up behind me. "It's for amateurs. You

should enter. I can teach you how to make muffins or something easy before next Friday. It would be fun to see you stretching out of your comfort zone."

I snorted. "This last year, I've been like a rubber band. Learning to be a witch from my snarky familiar has been a challenge. Toss in a few murders I helped solve, and I've been busy. Who's had time to learn to bake?" I gave her a side-eye. "Too bad one of my witchy skills wasn't in the kitchen." She knew I was referring to her particular specialty.

With a huge smile that showed off her pearly whites, she said, "We can't all be a kitchen witch. In fact, it's more rare than you think. Besides, you have skills I don't. The spell you cast with Dax to discover the secrets of the Heart of the Soul amulet, now that's something I could never have done."

With a shrug, "I guess that's what makes our coven so special. We're all different."

"Ladies," William came up behind us. "I see you've read the announcement. And forgive me, I couldn't help but overhear your conversation. Nikki's right, Lily. You should enter. I'd be happy to give you some tips, too. Cranberries are fairly easy to work with as long as you have enough sweetness to balance the tart."

Clasping my hands in front of me, I chewed the inside of my lip. Why couldn't I try my hand at baking? It wasn't like anyone would die from eating a muffin at a baking competition. Who knows, maybe I could surprise Gage by cooking something so he wouldn't have to be the primary chef after we tied the knot. I tapped my chin and scanned the poster again. "It says there are three rounds. I'm guessing that means the recipes will be more difficult with each round. I'd be thrilled if I made it through the first elimination."

William squeezed my shoulder reassuringly. "Lily, I've known you a long time. You can do anything you set your mind to. But remember, for this competition, there's no witchcraft. It has to be all non-magical. It's the only way it would be fair."

I patted his hand. "Even if you give me a few pointers, and Nikki too, I don't think I have a chance, but I'm willing to try."

"That's the spirit," he said. "Now I'll give you the sign-up sheet, and you can fill it out before you leave the shop." With a wiggle of his eyebrows, he said, "Plan on coming by tomorrow morning around eight. We'll have our first lesson in reading a recipe and correctly measuring ingredients."

Nikki draped her arm around my other shoulder. "I'll swing by your place tonight, and we'll practice by baking cookies."

The smiles on their faces didn't hide their excitement.

My mouth went dry, and my voice croaked. "Will they give me the recipes or a cookbook to follow?"

William frowned. "I hadn't thought of that. Nikki, we should choose several easy recipes that Lily can print out. I suspect most of the competitors will be experienced and create something off the top of their heads."

Her forehead wrinkled, and she paused before nodding. "Good idea."

For the second time, a shiver of nerves raced up and then down my spine. "You're making this sound more intimidating than facing down someone who's trying to kill me."

Nikki laughed. "Not at all. Between William and me, we'll have you ready to measure and mix with the best bakers in the county."

I knew she was being sweet. Nikki had seen some of my past baking disasters firsthand, but to William's point, I had been doing all kinds of things I would never have dreamt possible. With a deep exhale, I said, "I'm going to do this with your help. Before we even start to contemplate what comes next, I'm going to need sustenance—at least one cinnamon pecan roll and maybe even cookies to go with an extra-large coffee."

Being the best friend ever, Nikki said, "My treat, and let's not forget two chocolate croissants."

The sun was low in the sky, and it bathed my store in a golden light. I flopped into the wingback chair at the front of my shop. A whoosh escaped my lungs. "Nikki, how do you do this baking thing? Learning a spell is a snap compared to picking out recipes that I might be able to bake. And I use the word *might* with great reverence."

She closed the cookbook in her lap. Since I had to bake as a non-magical, we decided to scour cookbooks for recipes instead of the way Nikki baked with the combination of magic and hands-on experience. With a wink she said, "The best way to do anything well is to read the book."

I groaned. "Now you sound like Milo. Speaking of which, I wonder where the gray fur ball is snoozing." I got up and wandered around the shop, checking all his favorite napping zones. Finally, I saw the tip of his gray bushy tail lazily sliding from left to right over the carpet in the children's section. I knelt on the floor and peered under a little wooden chair. Reaching in, I ruffled the fur on his back.

In his typical kitty grumble, he said, "Go away. Can't you see I'm sleeping?"

My face split into a wide grin. "You're not, you're

talking to me. Besides you can't sleep the entire day away. What if I needed your help?"

He rolled to his side and looked at me through slits in his deep green eyes. "Do you?"

"As a matter of fact, yes. Join me and Nikki out front. I have news."

He lifted his head, and his eyes opened wider. "Another murder investigation? We've been in a nice groove lately; no one's bit the dust since Petra Addington."

"For once, I'm not trying to solve a murder." Milo was right; things had finally returned to a normal, sleepy town after we had eight suspicious deaths in the span of eighteen months. Coincidentally, the spate of murders and deaths had started when I discovered I was a witch. Not that I thought the events were related to each other.

I got up from the floor, brushed my hands on my jeans, and said, "Milo, come on out. Please."

Being a familiar came with certain expectations between a witch and her familiar. But my bond with Milo was far beyond what I had ever expected. He was my right hand, always ready to help me with anything, and that included the occasional human-interest puzzle as I liked to think of my part in solving crimes.

"Has Detective Cutie dropped by the shop today?"

I smiled as he used Gage's special nickname that few witches knew about. "No. With Dax moving to Robins Pointe, he's been extra busy. There's a new rookie cop, and training has fallen to Gage."

"That's right, I forgot about Peabody and Mac being promoted to detective." He crawled on his belly out from under the low-sitting chair and did a downward-facing dog stretch before moving into an arched-back cat stretch. He tipped his little head to the side and gave me a contemplative look. "How long are you going to hold me in suspense with this big news?"

I clasped my hands behind my back and rocked on the balls of my feet. "Not until you come out front."

He narrowed his eyes. "You are an exasperating witch. I wonder if I can appeal to the coven for a new one?"

"Ha. That's doubtful. You've said on more than one occasion we're connected forever."

"Don't remind me." He sat back on his haunches and swiped his paw over his face.

I bent over and scooped him into my arms. "Stalling time is over."

When I returned with Milo, Nikki put aside the cookbook she had been reading and said, "Where have you been hiding, little man?"

If a familiar could do a haughty sniff, it would be mine. "For your information, napping and hiding are not the same thing. If I had been doing the latter, Ms. Witch would never have found me."

I placed him on the upholstered chair. "Now, for my big surprise." I rubbed my hands together, trying to muster more enthusiasm than I felt. "I've entered a baking competition for next weekend. I would like your help in selecting a few recipes to have ready to bake. With some practice, I could possibly win this event."

"Wait. What. You. Bake?" He glared at Nikki. "You're encouraging this insanity. If anyone was going to enter, it should be you, and that win would be a lock."

Nikki said, "This is for nonprofessionals, and I happen to support Lily's attempt at broadening her skills in the kitchen."

"You'd better see what spells you can learn from *Practical Beginnings*."

He always resorted to bringing up my family's book of magic. "Milo, I have to do this the non-magical way, which is why I need your support. Now, we've selected several recipes. I'd like for you to take a look at what we have so far for muffins, cookies, cake, and even bread. Do you think they all sound good?" I took the stack of open cookbooks and held each one up for Milo to peruse. Thank the stars he could read. I didn't have to explain it all to him.

He snickered and murmured under his breath how there were some witches who should stay out of the kitchen except when opening a can of tuna and best suited to calling for takeout.

Tapping my foot while he took his sweet time, I wanted to remind him rude comments weren't needed. Instead, I chose to ignore his snark. He had to finish reading. To his credit, he nodded at a page in each book and only shook his head once. By the time I got to the final cook book, he had selected one of each variety.

After setting the last book aside, I said, "For the record, smarty pants, I have a few signature dishes that you've never complained about— roast chicken, fish, and scrambled eggs."

He nodded. "True, and Lily, I'm not complaining, much. You have other talents that Nikki doesn't have. Cooking just isn't your thing. The idea of you entering a baking competition has caught me off guard. As always, I'll do whatever is needed to support you." His tail swished from side to side. "And if by some quirk of fate, you do win, I'm expecting that very nice smoked salmon from Betty's Market. It will be adequate compensation for my assistance." He hopped from the chair to the floor. "When do lessons begin?"

"As soon as I close the shop. Nikki's coming over, and later Gage and Steve will be around for dinner." Nikki smiled when I mentioned her new husband. It still didn't seem right not to include Dax Peters in that statement. He was our friend and witch, who was more like family and formerly of Pembroke Cove. As of a few months ago, he was hired as the chief of police in Robins Pointe and was missed terribly when we got together for these impromptu meals.

Milo said, "I, too, miss Detective Sweet Tea."

I couldn't help but smile at Milo's nickname for Dax. "Hopefully, he can get away in the next few weeks and join us for some holiday cheer."

"If Nikki's baking, I'm sure he'll be around. That witch has a sweet tooth." He stalked from the room and, over his shoulder, said, "I'll see you at home."

I sank into the chair that Milo had vacated and gave Nikki a long look. "I know you encouraged me, but do you think I'm crazy for entering this contest? Milo's right. Even before I knew I was a witch, the kitchen was my least favorite room in the house."

She leaned forward and clasped my hand. "I know Gage does most of the cooking, but wouldn't it be nice to bake muffins or a pie for your handsome fiancé if you had the confidence to do it?"

I pointed to the stack of cookbooks we hadn't looked through yet. "Maybe we should find a couple of more recipes just to have enough flexibility for the contest."

She handed me a thick volume from off the stack.

"Nikki, please tell me you'll come to the event. I know we can't use magic, but with you in the room, it will be the moral support I need."

"Ogres couldn't keep me away." She squeezed my hand. "Gage, me, and everyone you love will be there cheering you on."

I hugged the cookbook to my chest and got up. With a sigh of determination, I said, "Well then, with everyone I love there, I'd better learn how to crack eggs without getting shells in the batter and cream butter, and I need to remember to include the cranberries."

Chapter 2
Lily

I couldn't tear my eyes away from Gage. We had just finished lunch and he held a forkful of pie midway between the plate and his mouth. Holding my breath, he took a bite. It was my most recent attempt, cranberry apple pie. After a week of baking every single night, I was either going to forget everything I had learned for the competition and potentially embarrass myself or make a respectable showing. "What do you think? Nikki suggested I make a sugar cookie-type crust to offset the tartness of the cranberries."

He bobbed his head from one side to the other. "The crust is quite good. Just the right amount of sweet but the filling," he paused and smacked his lips, "is rather tart. I'm not criticizing, but did you add enough sugar?"

I snatched the recipe card from the table and scanned the ingredient list before sinking into the chair next to him with a groan. "There's no sugar listed. I must have missed it when I copied over Nancy's recipe."

He picked through the filling, separating apples from

the cranberry mixture and the crust before he ate the apple bite with the tender bottom crust. "Sweetheart, you're on the right track. Just give Nancy a call before this afternoon and find out how much you need. Add it to your card, and you're golden."

My shoulders slumped. Defeat washed over me as my heart beat with a dull thud in my chest. "Let's face it, I can't be turned into a competitive baker in a few days. I'm going to withdraw. We can still go and cheer the others on."

Gage took my hand and tugged me into his lap. Wrapping his arms around me, he kissed my cheek. "I love the cookie crust, and I hope that you make the pie again. It's almost the best I've ever had." Holding out his thumb and index fingers that were a fraction of an inch apart, he said, "You're this close."

I took his fork and lopped off a bite. As soon as it was in my mouth, my face puckered. "Holy cow, that's sour." I looped my arms around his neck and pecked his lips. "This is just one of the many reasons why I'm marrying you."

"Because I'm your biggest cheerleader?"

"Nope." I brushed the lock of light brown hair that had fallen across his hazel eyes. "Your iron stomach." With one lingering kiss, I picked up the plate and stood. "I'm going to clean up and get ready to leave. I need to be at the town hall by two o'clock. They've set up stations with rows of ovens like what's in a bakery. I want to check out the space, and we have to bake something today."

"I'll help you clean up and go with you."

Placing my hand on his cheek, my heart felt as if it would overflow with love. "Another reason."

He pulled me into his arms. "Then set a date. Right here and now."

I opened my mouth and then closed it. "Not quite yet. I promise after the holidays, we'll pick a date and finalize plans for our wedding."

"Sounds good, and Lily, there's no pressure for our wedding. And about this baking event, I have seen you in action for most of my life. Whatever you set out to accomplish, you do. This contest won't be any different."

Wrapped in Gage's arms, I absorbed every bit of his confidence like a bone-dry sponge dropped into a basin of water. "Thank you." The words were simple, but there was so much more behind them. We had grown together, and as I supported him, he did the same for me.

Milo said, "If you two are done playing lovey-dovey, can we get going? I told some of my familiar gang that I'd meet them in front of the town hall before the big event starts."

Gage looked at my familiar perched on the chair. "Let me guess, Milo's trying to get you moving?"

I shrugged out of Gage's arms. "You know him so well." I scooped Milo up, gave him a hug and a kiss on the top of his soft furry head. "Please don't find any mischief today."

He swiveled his head like an owl and stared into my eyes. "Pot. Kettle. Enough said." He squirmed from my arms, dropped to the floor, and stalked out his kitty door. I heard him say as his tail disappeared, "I'll meet you at the car."

Gage and I strolled through the vestibule of the Pembroke Cove Town Hall. The main room had been transformed into a baking center for the event. To the right was a hallway that had been roped off and led to the town business offices. To the left were restrooms, and at the back were several closed doors typically used for small meetings and storage. The only areas that were open during the event were the latter.

Small groups of three to four people were clustered together around the perimeter of the community room. I wondered if each group had a baker and a cheering squad. My attention was drawn to Nikki waving from the back side of the room.

"Gage, look, there's Nikki, and she's found seats close to the baking centers."

We moved in that general direction, weaving through rows of chairs. To my left, I noticed a platform with a long banquet table and three chairs. *That must be for the judges.* As we drew closer, I noticed William and Jill Dilly sitting next to Steve, along with my parents, and Aunt Mimi and her husband Nate all had seats.

"Hey, you two. Here's the Lily Michaels contingent, and Gage, I saved two spots for your mom and dad, too."

I could feel my eyes widen. "Glenda and Burke are coming?" A heaviness filled my midsection. With all this support, I prayed I didn't make a fool out of myself.

Gage took my hand and gave it a squeeze. He leaned close. "You've proved countless times that you're fearless, holding your ground in front of killers and never giving up until the bad guys were behind bars. Don't let flour, sugar, and butter get the best of you." With a feather-like kiss on my lips, he whispered for my ears alone, "Believe in yourself as much as I do."

I straightened my shoulders, squeezed his hand in return, and crossed the room to the check-in table, leaving Gage with our friends and family.

Nancy Litchfield, my neighbor who generously gave me

her pie recipe, was there. A smile filled her face as she set aside her white and blue striped tote bag. "Lily Michaels. Are you ready to join in the fun?"

Wiping the palms of my hands on my jeans, I cleared my throat. Wasn't projecting confidence the first step in being a winner? "Hi, Nancy. I'm ready to check in." I leaned forward and whispered. "Thanks for the pie tips too, including the sugar."

"You're welcome." Her smile never faltered. She glanced around, but no one was close to us. "Have fun. After all, baking is just about taking a few ingredients and stirring them together into something tasty." She bobbed her head in the direction of the baking area. "Don't let some of these die-hard fanatics deflate you like a soufflé fresh from the oven."

I felt the color drain from my face. "I don't know how to make one. Should I have practiced that recipe too?"

She tapped the table in front of us. "I can't give away the details. You'll be given specific categories that your item must fit in, like quick bread, cake, and pies. You know, the typical kind of treat."

My breath evened out from the shallow breathing that had kicked in. "Whew. For a second I was starting to panic."

Nancy handed me a pink lanyard with a name tag. "You need to wear this when you're in the building today and tomorrow, and you're at station five on the right side, near your family."

"Thanks, Nancy. Are you a judge, too?"

"No, that's why I was comfortable giving you that recipe: there's no conflict of interest. But you have to promise to save me a slice if you make the cranberry apple pie."

My chest felt lighter with each passing sentence. "You got it."

"Would you like coffee or tea before we get started?" She nodded in the direction of the judges' table. I've been tasked with keeping them caffeinated."

Pressing my hand to my midsection, I said, "I don't need an additional stimulant to keep me on my toes. My nerves are working overtime."

I pivoted on my heels as a loud whistle shrieked from the direction of the raised dais. A short man, who was almost as wide as he was tall, stood on a stubby stool. "Can I have everyone's attention please? I'm Chef Julian Peppen. However, there's no relation to the famous chef Jacques Peppen. I'm an award-winning chef, having completed my training at the prestigious CIA in Hyde Park. No, I'm not a spy. That's the Culinary Institute of America, and if you've never heard of it, look it up." He laughed, and his belly shook like Jell-O under the white chef coat he wore. Rubbing his hands together, he smiled at Nancy, "Have all the participants checked in?"

She inclined her head forward, indicating yes. "Lily was the last to arrive."

That was surprising since I thought I had arrived early. *Everyone must be excited to get baking.*

"Excellent. If the bakers would take their spots," he paused and grinned widely, his apple cheeks almost obscuring his eyes. "I'll introduce the esteemed judges, review the rules, and then you can begin baking your first recipe."

I detected an edge in his voice as I hurried to my spot near my support team. Giving Gage and Nikki a grateful smile, I turned my full attention to Chef Julian.

The room was filled to capacity with spectators. Chairs

scraped over the wood floor as people moved to have a good view of the action in front of them. Chef Julian scanned the room. He crossed his arms and tapped the toe of his black loafers on the stool in rapid succession. Several minutes later, once the room was like a library, with the occasional hushed whisper, he turned to the group of ten bakers. I recognized several people from town— Daisy Patton, Frankie Thorn, and Dora Ingalls. Each one had a stellar reputation, and their baked goods were highly sought after when there were fundraising events. I rolled my neck from side to side, willing the roiling sensation in my tummy to stop.

A man took the spot next to me, held out his hand, and said, "Geoff Marks. I'm pleased to share a space with you."

My smile was guarded. Given the number of butterflies in my stomach, I was more worried I'd embarrass myself by stammering. Keeping it brief, I said, "Hello, Lily Michaels."

Chef Julian held up his hands. "Now for the judges. Besides myself, we have Roy Fletcher, a self-avowed foodie and roaming judge. The lovely and talented pastry chef, Blair Holt. She owns a string of bakeries up and down the East Coast, Sugar and Sprinkles. You might have heard of it."

Roy held up his white to-go coffee cup and grinned. Blair did the same with her water bottle as she gave a nod to all.

A murmur rippled throughout the room. It was hard to tell if it was good or bad.

Chef Julian wrapped his knuckles on the cluttered tabletop. It had only taken a few minutes for it to become overfilled with bottles of water, white disposable coffee cups, three white pastry boxes, and clipboards. He held up his hand. "Pay attention, bakers. This is critical. We have a couple of food allergies. No almonds, peanuts, cinnamon, or red dye can be used in any of your recipes, and no artificial sweeteners of any kind. We want your baked goods to be in the purest form possible. For your first creation, you have exactly one hour. Of course, as you already know, the theme is everything cranberry. It must be a key ingredient in the muffins you'll bake. You can use any ingredients you find on the shelves behind you, but you are *not* permitted to use anything you brought with you. After all, this needs to be a fair competition." With a snide grin, he added, "And do the judges a favor by being creative. The quickest way out the door is to turn in a muffin I could find in a grocery store bakery." He tapped the small bell to his right. "You may begin."

People rushed to the bakers' racks while I withdrew the laminated recipe cards from my pocket. I inhaled and exhaled, hoping to steady my quivering hands. The last thing I needed was to mix the batter and have it splatter all over the counter because I couldn't control the whisk. I laughed to myself at the complete over-exaggeration. Even if I was questioning my sanity for jumping into this event with both feet. The rush of bakers to and from the shelves was over. I reviewed what I needed and withdrew the basket from under the counter. It would be one trip, and I'd be whisking momentarily.

I was plating my muffins as the three-minute warning timer dinged. I didn't dare look at anyone else's progress since I was sure I was dead last. But that didn't matter. I'd baked muffins with golden brown tops and dots of glistening ruby-red fruit peeking through. The final bell clanged, and like the other bakers, I dropped my arms to my sides and stepped back from my counter to await what came next.

Chef Julian rose to his feet. "Bakers, you've accomplished the first part of any good cooking competition, filling the air with delectable aromas. Nancy will pass out small plastic plates to each one of you. They'll have your initials on the underside. Place a single muffin on three plates and take a seat. We'll announce the results once we've tasted and scored them." He plunked to his seat with a grunt.

Nancy walked down the row of baking stations, handing each contestant a stack of plates. I took mine and placed three of the best-looking muffins on them. Once Nancy took my plates, I leaned hip-first against the counter. I stole a glance in the direction of my cheering section. Gage winked. Nikki gave me two thumbs up, and my parents were beaming like I had just taken my first baby steps. The minutes ticked by as I gave my full attention to the judges. Roy Fletcher was pulling at the collar of his turtleneck sweater, his face flushed crimson. When they got to my muffin, each judge broke off a piece and popped it in their mouth. Roy nodded and said something to Chef Julian and Blair. She glanced in my direction before jotting something on the paper in front of her. Since I was the last entry, the results should be announced shortly.

Ten minutes later, after Chef Julian jotted a note on the clipboard, he rose to his feet and brushed crumbs off the front of his coat. I didn't like his self-important persona, but that didn't matter. I wasn't here to become his best friend.

"After careful consideration, we have decided to change the posted rules; this is a nonelimination round. I'm pleased to announce that Dora Ingalls has taken first place with her Leftover Cranberry Sauce Oatmeal Muffins." He clapped his hands together. "Well done, Dora."

Everyone clapped as the older woman beamed.

"In second place," Chef Julian continued, "is Geoff Marks with his Cranberry White Chocolate Muffins, and in third place is Lily Michaels with her entry, Dried Cranberry Pecan Streusel Muffins."

I placed a hand on my chest, and my mouth gaped open. Had I heard Chef Julian correctly? I was actually in third place for the contest. I began to turn to Nikki when, from the corner of my eye, I saw Roy slump like a wet lasagna noodle from his chair to the dais and then to the floor. He landed with a soft thud.

Gage sprang to his feet. He snaked his way through the people who had stood to have a better view. "Police officer coming through."

I rushed around the back of the baking station, weaving around the contestants, clutching my cell phone in my hand. Gage was kneeling next to Roy after he had rolled him to his back.

"Lily, call for the EMTs. I think he's had a heart attack or an allergic reaction." He pressed his fingers to the side of Roy's neck. "He's got a pulse, but it's weak." He cradled Roy's shoulders and tipped back his head. "Does anyone have an EpiPen?"

A murmur rippled through the crowd, but no one came forward.

I noticed Roy's lips were blue-gray and his skin deathly pale. I could hear the poor man wheezing as he struggled for each breath.

Burke, Gage's dad, slipped his hands under Roy's arms and lifted him to a partial sitting position. "Gage, look at the size of his tongue. It's definitely anaphylaxis. Mimi might be able to help get him stabilized before it's too late."

"Aunt Mimi?" I touched the base of my throat to amplify my voice so it carried above the din. Silently thanking the stars for having learned that spell just last week. Sometimes Milo was right and I needed to proactively read my book. I scanned the room. Nate was in front of her, heading in our direction. The onlookers parted like asphalt after an earthquake, jagged but wide.

When she reached my side, she took a look at Roy on the floor. "Lily, what's going on?"

"We think it's an allergic reaction. Can you help?"

Her petite frame was dwarfed as she sandwiched herself between Gage and Burke. Placing her palm on his chest, I could see her mouth moving but couldn't hear the words she said. Aunt Mimi was a witch and the best healer I knew. She saved Milo's life a few months ago and healed me on several occasions, too. If anyone could help Roy Fletcher, it was her. I took a step back and stuck my hands in the jacket hanging off the back of the chair he had been in just moments before. My only discovery, lint balls.

A siren's wail pierced the air. It seemed like seconds, as Suzi and Stew, two of the town's best emergency personnel, dropped medical cases with a thud. Suzi tapped Burke on the shoulder so she could get closer. "What's the situation?"

Stew started his physical assessment by placing a stethoscope on Roy's chest. "How long has he been like this?"

I said, "He collapsed less than fifteen minutes ago."

He strapped on the blood pressure cuff and pumped it up repeatedly, placing his fingers on the underside of Roy's wrist. "Does anyone know if he has food allergies?"

"Chef Julian said the judges have allergies, but I'm not sure what Roy is specifically allergic to. All that was mentioned was nuts, red dye, and cinnamon. Oh, and artificial sweeteners."

Stew gave a slow shake of his head. "This is a severe reaction." Suzi handed him what looked like an oversized lipstick case with one end bright orange. Stew placed it against Roy's thigh and pressed down.

I held my breath, waiting for Roy to take a normal breath. Was that even possible this quickly after a dose of medicine? I felt a rush of sadness that he was deathly sick. The only upside, it wasn't murder this time.

Chapter 3
Gage

My face felt hot as I sat back on my heels. Stew and Suzi strapped Roy Fletcher to the stretcher and elevated it for ease of navigation out of the building. My newly promoted detectives, Sharon Peabody and Mac Sullivan, had arrived and were at the entrance. Their arms were stretched wide, holding the crowd back to give the EMTs plenty of room. Several uniformed officers were separating people into smaller groups for questioning before releasing them.

"Gage?" Lily had her hands in her apron pockets. "What can I do to help?"

I slipped my arm around her waist and kissed her temple. Taking a moment to savor the smell of sweet muffins that clung to her clothes. "You can give a statement to Peabody and then go home."

She frowned. "Not likely. A man ingested a substance that almost killed him right in front of us. I'm more help to you if I wander around and see if I can overhear any snippets of conversations." Tapping her fingertip to her nose. "There's more to this than a simple mistake."

On the one hand, she was right that she could mingle and probably learn more than I would in my official capacity. But history had proven every time she got involved with someone dying in less-than-expected circumstances, she usually wound up in a pickle. Not that she didn't have the skills as a witch to protect herself. I hesitated. The help would be nice. In addition, I learned that it was easier to give her something to do than expect her to walk away. She'd just find her way back anyway.

Thank heavens Roy wasn't dead and I hoped I wasn't going to regret this. "You can help on a couple of conditions."

Her eyes widened as if she hadn't expected me to agree so quickly. "Anything."

"If you find something, don't touch it, tell me. If you hear something, don't ask questions, let me know. Basically, stroll through the crowd, be an extra set of eyes and ears for me."

She held up her pinky finger and crooked it around mine. "Got it. For everything I might discover, let you know."

Her eyes locked on to something or someone behind me. I turned to see if I could tell what she had focused on. "Lily, don't question Chef Julian. I'll have Peabody or Mac tackle him."

"Oh, don't worry. I won't, but he might know if Roy had any specific allergies. And... I'm going to peruse the baking racks just to make sure the ingredients that Julian mentioned aren't sitting on a shelf." She eased out of the circle of my arm and made a beeline for the judge's platform. Julian Peppen and Blair Holt were sitting in their chairs, with vacant stares. I waited until Lily crossed the room before speaking with Mac and Peabody.

"Thanks for coming, Detectives." They had been excellent police officers and would be just as good in their new roles.

"Detective Erikson, can you tell us what happened?" Peabody's clipped tone sounded like she was questioning a suspect and not her superior.

Overlooking her brusque manner, I said, "The judges had just finished the first round of sampling. Right after Lily's name was announced as the third-place winner, Roy fell from his chair to the floor. I got to him as fast as I could. His pulse was very weak, his tongue swollen, and I suspect he was close to dying."

"Any theory as to what caused him to collapse?" she asked.

"An allergic reaction is the current hypothesis." I nodded in Lily's direction. "Guess who's going to do a little sleuthing for us?"

Peabody's smile escaped her work mask. "I suspect she'll turn up something before we do. She has a talent for observation and can do so under the guise of a participant."

I groaned. "Don't remind me. Do me a favor, keep an eye on her, just in case someone gets upset with her discreet inquiries."

"You mean like Chef Julian?" Mac said. "He's a piece of work. I was surprised when I heard he was a judge with Blair Holt. They've had a long-running feud. Rumor has it that something happened with her signature pumpkin pie a couple of years ago, or maybe it had something to do with his cookbook. I'm not sure now."

I clapped my hand on Mac's shoulder. "Not our issue today. We have to get these people questioned and released in an expeditious manner. As soon as I hear from the emergency room doctor, I'll let you know Roy's condition. At least we don't have to call EL in this time."

At the mention of the town coroner, Peabody's cheek flushed an interesting shade of pink. "Actually, I want to check in with Lily. Peabody, can you give him a call? Ask him about anaphylactic shock, and if Roy Fletcher's in a coma, how likely is it that he'll come out of it." I knew I was jumping to a conclusion but better to have more information than less.

"You've got it, Detective."

I wasn't going to remind her again it was okay to call me Gage. She had gotten into the habit when she was a police officer, and the same with Mac. Now that we were a similar rank, I wished we could be a bit less formal on the job. Trying to find that same rhythm with them as I had with my former partner, Dax Peters, was going to take time.

As I waded through the crowd, I noticed my parents and Lily's off to one side. Nikki and Steve were talking with one of the officers. I didn't see William and Jill. I made a detour to check in with the parents.

"Hey folks. How's everyone?"

My dad spoke up first. "We're fine, just waiting our turn to share what we saw with the police. Which wasn't much. We were focused on Lily whipping up her winning muffins."

A smile crept over my face. "Can you believe she got third place?"

Lily's dad, Reed, nodded. "Her aunt Mimi's recipe is unbeatable."

"Where are Mimi and Nate?" I scanned the room and didn't see them. "I wanted to talk with her."

"They were among the first to be questioned. I would

guess they're either on their way to their house or chatting with William and Jill outside," Reed said.

My eyes followed Lily as she glanced over her shoulder and pointed to where the baking ingredients were stored. "Will you excuse me? I'm curious to see what my fiancée has discovered." I didn't wait for anyone to answer as I hurried after Lily. Even from this distance, I knew that gleam in her eye, and it meant she was on the trail of something specific.

Our eyes met, and she winked. "I had a hunch. Unfortunately, it hasn't panned out."

"Care to fill me in?" I asked as I reached her side.

She gestured to the racks in front of us. "I was looking for some ingredients. Do you remember how Chef Julian said we couldn't use almonds, cinnamon, peanuts, or sugar substitutes when he was giving us the rules?"

I shook my head. "To be honest, I wasn't paying much attention to what he said. I was concentrating on you and sending you soothing vibes. From where I was sitting, I could see your hands trembling."

With a soft laugh, she agreed. "I thought maybe I'd find peanuts or a big bottle of cinnamon since it's a common spice. Those items could have gotten on the shelves by mistake. But there's nothing. I'm going to check each baking station, too. We weren't supposed to bring any ingredients, but you never know."

"Maybe I should question the remaining two judges to see what allergies they might have and ask if they knew what Roy was allergic to."

Lily turned me in the direction of Julian and Blair. She whispered in my ear. "Let me know what you find out. I'm going to keep looking here."

I pulled myself up to my full height. I wanted to project

the don't mess with the detective attitude since Julian was full of himself and Blair ... who knew what she thought. To my knowledge, the judge hadn't said more than a few words. All she seemed to do was smile and nod.

Julian pointed to me and said something to Blair as I approached. Her expression never changed from the look of a bored person at a party. I wondered how she could be so cool and collected, considering someone had almost died mere feet from her. But hey, it took all kinds.

"Hello. We haven't officially met. I'm Detective Gage Erikson of the Pembroke Cove Police Department. I have a couple of questions."

Julian jabbed a finger in the direction of the uniformed officers. "Isn't that *their* job?"

It was hard to overlook his snarky tone. He wasn't the first person to be annoyed at being detained by me nor would he be the last. "Well, if talking to me speeds things up and gets you out the door, all the better, right?"

"Oh, we won't be leaving. We're in the middle of a bake-off. Blair and I've talked it over, and we agree we're going to pick up right where we were. Get the contestants cooking. It will get their minds off the unpleasantness. I'm sure that's what Roy would have wanted."

That segue couldn't have lined up more perfectly for my questions. "I was hoping you could clarify a few things. Julian, you mentioned four ingredients couldn't be used. Who's allergic to what?"

"Blair is allergic to nuts, I can't stand anything with almond flour, it's a texture thing for me, and Roy hated the taste of cinnamon. In an effort to give everyone the best chance to win, we just put it out there: allergies. No sense in someone preparing a cranberry coffee cake with cinnamon and Roy rating it with poor marks just because he refuses to taste it." He leaned forward. "I can't believe anyone doesn't like cinnamon in baked goods but our differences make the world go around."

"Blair, you're allergic to nuts? Do you mind telling me what happens if you accidentally ingest them?"

She patted the right side of her leather jacket and then the left. Her face paled. "I don't leave home without my EpiPen. It's a literal lifesaver." She grabbed her bag from the floor and dumped it on the table. Pushing around the contents she whispered, "But mine's gone."

"You're just discovering this now. I called out if anyone had one with them, and you never said a word."

Blair's face scrunched up. "I, I must not have heard you with all the confusion."

I let that comment pass for now. "You are severely allergic to all nuts or just almonds?"

She crossed her arms and legs and only gave me a glancing look. "Peanuts are technically a legume. They don't grow on trees. Per my allergy testing, it's just almonds and almond butter. I carry an EpiPen at all times since I've discovered even when I think a food item is safe, it might have been prepared near the nuts. It's not worth taking the chances."

I nodded. "Good to know." Looking out over the thinning crowd, I said, "Do you know if Roy had any allergies?"

"We're not married to the man and only know what he told us," Julian laughed.

Blair crossed her arms over her chest and looked away from Julian. "You're rude, and he's our friend. The poor man is deathly ill, and you're cracking jokes at his expense. How typical."

Julian's smile melted. "Do you have something that you're dying to say to me?"

She sniffed and turned in her chair so her back was to him. "Nothing new. You've been a cold and callous human all the years I've known you. Why I thought anything would have changed is beyond me."

Color rose from his collar to his hairline. "Blair. Now is not the time to bring up ancient history."

"Ha!" She spun around and jabbed her index finger into his chest. "I told you when I discovered those dead rats in my Portland facility that you'd pay for what you did. I never forget or go back on my word."

Now, this was an interesting exchange, but it was irrelevant to Roy Fletcher's collapse. "Please, let's get back to the current situation."

Julian glared at Blair. "We'll discuss this later."

"Over my dead body." Each word was punctuated with a poke into his chest.

He grabbed her hand. "That can be arranged."

"Mr. Peppen. It's a crime to threaten another with bodily harm. Ms. Holt, would you like to press charges?"

She wrenched her hand from Julian and rubbed where he had squeezed it. "No. I think our tempers are running hot due to Roy. It's not every day you're with someone when they collapse." She rose from the chair. "I forgive you, Julian." As she moved away, she murmured so that I could almost hear her clearly. "But this isn't over."

"Can you believe her? After ten years of feuding, we should both wind up here judging this contest. What are the odds?"

I watched as Blair Holt strolled behind the baking stations in Lily's direction. She had been observing the exchange between the judges, and she was definitely about to ask a few discreet questions to learn more. I was curious about the conversation and wondered if I needed to learn more about the barely restrained hostility between these two.

"Chef, you weren't aware who the other judges were before arriving at the event?"

"I wasn't. Not that Lois Vanderhaven, the town manager, had to clear it with me, but I wish she had given me a heads-up. I liked Roy. A talented amateur baker, but Blair Holt is another story. A vile woman who claims I am out to ruin her pathetic chain of bakeries. She's expanded so fast she's forgotten a quality product is more important than quantity. It's no wonder she got rats."

I sat quietly, waiting for Julian to continue. I had discovered a long time ago that when someone had information they might want to get off their chest, it was best to give them the time to do so.

"Like I would steal her award-winning recipes and publish them in my cookbooks. Who needs to poach from a second-rate chef? I trained in Paris under some of the greatest pastry chefs in the world." He snorted and rapped the top of the folding table with his knuckles, causing it to sway from the force. "Something needs to be done about her. Maybe the world will get lucky, and she'll croak from a heart attack."

"Julian, might I remind you that making a veiled threat is still a threat?"

He held up the palms of his hands in surrender. "Look, I'm all talk and zero action. Just ask anyone. There are plenty of people that will vouch for me."

I opened my mouth to say something when I heard Lily call to me. "Gage, can you come here a moment please?"

I kept one eye on Lily and said to Chef Julian, "Excuse me, and don't go anywhere. I'll be back, and we will finish this conversation."

Chapter 4
Lily

Blair Holt had spilled her guts in under five minutes before saying she needed a breath of air. As she walked out the door, I called to Gage. I considered the feud between the remaining two judges but, more so, how she had mentioned that Roy and Julian were best buds. Together, they wanted to destroy her business.

"Did you find something?" Gage asked.

"Not yet, but did you know that Roy and Julian are tight? And according to Blair they've been trying to put her out of business for years."

"That's interesting. Julian is acting like they are mere acquaintances, nothing more. I guess I'd better dig a little deeper. This situation might not have been an accident. I wonder if Blair was taking the opportunity for a little payback."

"Have you heard from the hospital about Roy's condition? I've never seen or heard anyone make that rattling sound."

"Mimi seemed to help ease his breathing before the EMTs arrived, and with the administration of the EpiPen, it has to have helped. He must have been feeling the effects while he was sitting on the dais."

I snapped my fingers. "Before he sampled my muffins, I saw his face getting red, and he pulled on the collar of his sweater. I'll bet he was having trouble breathing then. Any idea how long it takes for a reaction to happen?"

"I can't answer that question, but Peabody is talking with EL to get some details." Gage nodded in her direction. "Do you notice anything interesting?"

Sharon was smiling while she was talking on the phone, and her cheeks were flushed a charming shade of pink. "You didn't tell me those two were an item."

"I don't know that they are. When I mentioned him earlier, she got that same look on her face that she has now."

"Maybe we should get some people together and invite both of them. If they're not dating yet, maybe they need a little nudge."

"My darling witch, please don't start trying to be a matchmaker on top of your other accomplishments." Gage kissed my cheek. "Oh, and Chef Julian says you're going to be baking again today. Take a last look around and be ready to pick up your whisk again."

"Thanks for the heads-up." Withdrawing my cell phone I added, "I'm going to take pictures of every workstation before the bakers come back. Then I can study them later."

"Take pictures of the baking racks too. Just to be thorough."

I tapped my temple and the corner of my mouth tipped up in a smile. "I'm one step ahead of you, detective."

"You always are." He touched my hand as he moved in Mac's direction.

I watched him walk away and sighed with a profound sense of contentment. Despite what had happened to poor Roy, having Gage here when it occurred was calming.

Quickly scanning the location of each contestant, I began to take a multitude of pictures for each of the nine spaces. For good measure, I went back and did one more set of images of the spice rack. If Roy was allergic to cinnamon, there had to be a bottle here.

Thirty minutes later, what was left of the people in the audience were back in their seats. I was in my station along with the rest of the bakers. The audience was settled in, and once again, Chef Julian and Blair were sitting at the judge's table. In Roy's place was Fred Wickshire, the owner of one of the town's favorite eateries, the Clam Bake. Chef Julian held up his hand, and everyone seemed riveted by what he was about to say.

"Thank you, everyone, for your patience during our little emergency. Roy Fletcher is in good hands at the hospital. When we get an update on his condition, I'll pass along the information. Until then, I'd like to introduce Fred Wickshire, who has graciously agreed to fill in for Roy. On a positive note, Fred has zero food allergies."

The restaurant owner squirmed in his chair and looked at the table. Chef Julian rubbed his hands together, which I was beginning to find mildly annoying. Once was more than enough.

"Your next challenge is to make a cookie that pairs perfectly with a cup of coffee on a crisp fall day. You will have ninety minutes in case someone needs to refrigerate their dough before baking." He looked down the length of the table and gave Blair and Fred a knowing grin. "Baking begins now."

This time, he clanged an oversized whisk against a coffee mug. I didn't wait for the others to get their items. If I was going to finish baking cranberry biscotti on time, every second counted. It was a great cookie that was a big seller at the Sweet Spot and my personal favorite. William mentioned it always took more than ninety minutes. I didn't dare look at Nikki or my family. I was sure this time I'd disappoint them, but I was going all in and try my best.

Silently, I was thankful I had spent time perusing the shelves. I had a good idea of where I'd find the pastry flour and other ingredients. I put my hand on a jar of pistachio nuts; with Blair having a nut allergy, I changed my mind and grabbed the coconut and green colored sugar instead. That would make a festive touch once I dipped the biscotti in the melted chocolate.

Once I had my ingredients assembled in front of me, I whisked the butter and sugar together until fluffy, remembering each helpful tip Nikki gave me. I combined the dry ingredients with the wet, shaped them into loaves, put them on parchment paper, and slipped the baking sheets into the oven. Victorious, I set the timer.

Dang it! I whipped them out and dropped the sheets on the counter, shaking my hands at the heat from the pans. At least they were just getting hot. But the dough needed to be refrigerated first. I flicked off the oven, transferred the parchment and dough to cold cookie sheets, and slid them into the stainless steel refrigerator behind me.

Daisy gave me a reassuring smile. "It's okay, Lily, don't let a tiny bump derail you; you're doing great."

"Thanks, Daisy, that's really sweet of you. What are you baking?" I wasn't sure if I could leave my area, so I stood on my tiptoes to get a better look.

"Cranberry rosemary thumbprint cookies. I'm not sure

how they'll turn out. I always use cinnamon in the dough, and since we have allergies, I've had to modify things, including the cranberry filling."

"I'm sure they'll be amazing. I never thought about a thumbprint cookie."

She flashed me a grin. "I'm glad one of us is confident. I'm going to drizzle white chocolate over the top. I'll save you one if you'd like to try them?"

"Sure, and if my biscotti is edible, I'll save you one too."

Geoff Marks laughed. "Ladies, you're not sounding like competitors in a baking contest but old friends getting ready for a cookie swap. I'm here to win. Don't count on sampling anything that I make."

Dora looked up from the mixing bowl she held close to her body. With a flicker of a smile, she said, "If you're baking your signature cookie, oatmeal cranberry, you have nothing to worry about. Store bought cookies have more flavor."

I was shocked at how these bakers got testy with each other. But I guess bragging rights and a couple hundred bucks put some people into a highly competitive state. All I wanted was to say I participated, and I'd done just that. I didn't expect to win but then I thought of my muffin entry and it won third place. Even if I was a novice, it didn't mean I couldn't produce a decent sweet treat.

My timer went off. I pulled the dough out of the refrigerator, slid the parchment back to the original pans, and finally, my dough was baking for the next thirty minutes. Cool, cut, and bake again, and then I'd dip the finished product in chocolate and plate it. I glanced at the clock and bit my lower lip. I had barely enough time left to finish. Nothing else could go wrong.

Gage held up his phone in my direction and headed to

the back of the room. Since I was killing time anyway, I hurried after him.

Just as I got there, Gage said, "Thanks for calling, EL. I appreciate the information."

I held out my hand so I could take the phone. He quirked a brow, shook his head, then handed it to me.

"EL, this is Lily. How are you?"

"Fine, thank you. Congratulations. I heard you made it through the first round."

"Yes, it's going well." I had dough to get back to so I said, "Listen, Gage and I are going to have some people over tomorrow night for lasagna. Don't worry I'm not cooking but would you like to come? It'll be super cas, you know, just a few friends." Hopefully, the invitation came off breezy and casual.

"I wouldn't want to..." he began.

"EL, I wouldn't have extended the invite if we didn't want you there. Please say you'll join us. Or better yet, I won't take no for an answer. Come any time after five thirty. Bye now." I didn't bother to wait for him to respond.

I handed the phone back to Gage and quickly made a list of who needed to be invited. I was confident I'd convince Nikki to whip up a large pan of lasagna and dessert. I could handle salad. Now, scanning the room, I wondered where Sharon Peabody was.

Gage had slipped the phone into his jeans pocket when he leaned close. "Daisy's waving frantically. Is she trying to get your attention?"

I glanced at my watch. The timer wasn't due to go off on my cookies, yet she was obviously distraught. "If you see Sharon, let her know I need to speak with her, and when you get back to your seat, let Nikki and Steve know we're hosting dinner tomorrow night."

"Sweetheart, you really shouldn't be getting involved in people's love lives."

With a wave of my hand, I said, "Nonsense." A feeling of dread began to settle in the pit of my stomach. Daisy's smile had faded as she pointed to my oven. I picked up the pace and scurried around the end of the counter.

"Lily, I took a peek in your oven since you were in the back of the room. I don't think your oven is actually working. There's no heat coming out when I opened the door and the dough looks raw."

Had I forgotten to turn it back on? Tears pricked my eyelids. Wasn't it like me to mess up baking something as simple as a cookie? Now, what was I going to do?

Daisy pointed to an oven behind us. "Use that one. It's a convection oven. Keep the temperature twenty-five degrees lower than the regular, and it bakes in less time, too."

What did I have to lose? I transferred the baking pans into the other oven and crossed my fingers as I looked to the heavens. I wasn't ready to go home from this competition. I had Nancy's pie to bake.

When I looked at where Gage should be sitting, I saw his chair was vacant. While searching the spacious room, I noticed he was talking to Mac and Sharon. Their faces were grim. Did it mean that poor Roy Fletcher had died after they got him to the hospital?

My eyes never left them. Gage looked at me. I breathed a sigh of relief when he didn't give me a thumbs down. I took that as Roy was still holding on.

"Bakers, thirty minutes," Chef Julian announced.

I could get ahead of the curve by setting up my chocolate dipping and decorating station. Thinking that this was something Nikki did every day, I had to wonder why. Even as a witch, baking was hard work. She needed to know all those spells and what the best flavor combinations were. It took a skill set that I wasn't willing to cultivate after this weekend.

Finally, Chef Julian rapped a mallet on the tabletop. "Bakers, whisks down. It's time to see how the cookie crumbles." He laughed more to himself. "I always wanted to say that in a contest, and now I have."

My plate of cookies didn't look appetizing. If I didn't make it to the next round of the competition, that would put much less pressure on me and give me more time to observe others around me. Like, what did Roy ingest to go into anaphylactic shock?

We went through the same process as before. The judges announced Dora in first place and Daisy Patton in second, and I tied with Frankie Thorn in third. I still didn't know what he had submitted. I was shocked. There was no way my cookie was good enough to get third place.

Geoff Marks shouted, "This is rigged and outrageous."

Chef Julian tipped the mallet in Geoff's direction and narrowed his eyes. "You have an honorable mention, so you'll move on to the next round." He nodded at the other five bakers. "The rest of you will be going home. Try again at the next competition and keep working on your recipes. Cooking, like all good things, takes practice and skill."

A few people grumbled, but the others just picked up their bag of tools and walked out of the cooking area single file.

I looked across the baking area and locked my knees so they'd continue to hold me upright and swallowed the lump in my throat. And now there were five.

Chapter 5
Lily

Geoff shook his clenched fist at me, his face turning a deep shade of purple. "What do you mean Lily Michaels's cookies came in third? Just look at them. They don't even look like they were fully baked."

My mouth dropped open, and my eyes popped. Apparently, I wasn't good at masking my surprise at his outburst, but he had a point. The biscotti didn't look appetizing compared to several of the other contestants' cookies.

Blair said, "If I may." She gestured to the row of plates in front of the judges. "We specifically asked for cookies. Anything that is not a cookie, which by definition is something to be eaten with your fingers, is automatically disqualified. We have tarts, cupcakes, and turnovers which need to be eaten with a fork. For the record, I can't wait to try one, but they're not cookies. We had four cookies from which to select the best. Lily and Frankie tied for third place. Geoff, you should have elevated your cookie submission if you wanted to be a contender."

He glared at Blair. "The texture of my white chocolate oatmeal cookie is perfect."

"Yes, but that is only one factor. Taste is critical."

"Enough of this banter." Chef Julian tapped the face of his watch. "Considering all the interruptions we've had today and the near miss with Lily's oven, I suggest we postpone the rest of the competition until tomorrow at ten o'clock, and that's in the morning, people. Starting fresh might be what we all need."

Geoff spun on his heel and grabbed his stack of laminated recipe cards. Without saying goodbye to anyone, he stormed from the baking center.

I looked at Dora and Daisy. "Is he always like that?"

Daisy shrugged. "I've only met him at one other event. He's from Drake's Bay, and his behavior is typical of what I saw the last time we met in a competition. Geoff thinks he's some hotshot baker, but he takes shortcuts and doesn't layer flavors into anything he makes.

That caught my attention. "Do you enter these contests often?"

Daisy smiled. "Yes. I keep hoping if I come out as the grand prize winner. It'll help me put together a portfolio for an angel investor to open my own bakery."

"That's great, Daisy. Have you thought about talking to Blair? Would she be able to help you?"

Her smile morphed into a frown. "That one? Every time I see her at one of these events, she looks down on most of us like we're kids playing with an Easy Bake Oven."

That was the opening I needed. "Is it usually the same judges in the northeast? Chef Julian, Roy, and Blair?"

"Most of the time. I know what Julian said before, and he made it sound like this was a rare occurrence. But he lied. And don't trust him. He's a snake without a built-in warning system. If you catch my drift."

"What about Roy? Is he a good guy, or does he fall in the same category as Julian or Blair for that matter?"

She licked her lips. "He's pretty quiet, keeps to himself but fair. Although I get the impression that Julian can sway him if necessary."

I stood up straighter. "Oh. What happened?" I needed to be careful with what I asked her. The last thing I wanted to do was put her guard up by asking all kinds of questions that she might interpret I was angling to get the inside track to win the competition.

She tipped her head and gave me a thoughtful look. "One time, there was what appeared to be a three-way tie for the grand prize winner. That time I was just a spectator and not a participant. The judges, Blair, Julian, and Roy, were working that event. When it came time to announce the winner it seemed each one picked a different person from the three that were left. Julian pulled Roy aside, and it was quite a heated exchange. When they came back to the table, Roy's shoulders were slumped, and it was easy to see he was about to change his vote. Blair's face went scarlet, and I overheard her say if he couldn't stand by his decision, he shouldn't be a judge."

"Really?"

"And that's not all. After that, they changed the rules so that there were two finalists, not three. This way a tie isn't possible."

I had been expecting a juicy detail and felt let down like it was an obvious thing to do. "Stabbing in the dark, I guess Roy changed his vote to Julian's choice?"

"You guessed right." Daisy gathered up her notebook, a

few baking tools on her workstation, and two small vials and slipped them into her tote bag.

She noticed me looking at the containers. "Oh, it's not what you think. I always bring aspirin and antacids to these events. Do you need to take something?" She opened one of the vials, and I saw it was as she said.

"No. I'm good." I was disappointed it was a dead end.

With a flutter of her fingers, she said, "Toodles. See you tomorrow."

By this time, I was the only contestant left. Julian and Fred were casually chatting at the judges' table and Blair was nowhere to be found.

My personal cheerleaders were in the same spot as before, but Gage was looking in my direction. I forced a smile but didn't really feel it. Was I missing something about Roy's collapse? The entire event felt off. Gage withdrew from the group and headed in my direction.

Slipping his arm around my waist, he pulled me close. "I know that wrinkle between your eyes. What's troubling you?"

"Do you think it's possible that Roy was intentionally slipped something he was allergic too?"

"Funny you should bring that up. I heard from the hospital. Roy definitely ingested something, and he was deathly allergic to it. It could have been early in the day, or right up until he sampled the muffins."

I thought back to when they first sat down. "What happened to Roy's coffee cup? Remember when he was introduced, he held it up in a cheers motion."

"I don't." He took my hand and urged me in the direction of the judges' table.

It was littered with plates of cookies, empty water bottles, and several coffee cups, but they weren't the to-go version that Roy had. They had the logo from the Copper Kettle just down the street.

A large gray trash barrel overflowing with remnants of the day was pushed against the back wall. My brow arched when I looked at Gage.

He shook his head. "I know that gleam in your eye. We're not going through a barrel of trash."

"How else are we going to find the cup that Roy brought in? It could hold the key to his health problem."

He pointed to my ankle booties, black jeans, and pretty cardigan I wore. "You want to get this outfit soiled with that mess?"

"No. But you can guard it, and I'll run home and change."

He withdrew his cell phone. "I'll call the station and have someone pick it up. We can have a couple of officers or even Sharon and Mac sort it out and find the cup. But it will be like looking for a wand in a haystack. Who knows. The cup could have been tossed anywhere else."

"Right, like if someone was trying to kill him and during the confusion when he collapsed, they slip in, take the cup with them, and boom, evidence vanishes."

"Lily, we don't have anything to prove it was a deliberate act either."

I playfully shook my finger in his direction. "And we don't have anything proving it wasn't. Julian said he wasn't allergic to cinnamon. He just didn't like it. We need to find out if that's the truth. Do you plan on talking to Roy?"

"I wish I could. He's in a coma, and the doctor doesn't know when or if he'll come out of it."

I clutched his arm. "You're joking. Just a few hours ago, he was smiling and voting for my muffins. Now, he might die?"

"It's a possibility. The doctor doesn't know for sure."

He dialed his cell, and I waited while he requested someone come over and gather all the trash. After explaining that Roy had arrived with a to-go coffee cup and that it should be tested to determine if the coffee had been spiked with anything, he disconnected.

Making a beeline to my family, I briefly told them that Gage and I were going to hang out for a bit. I kissed my mom and dad's cheeks, saying, "Thanks for coming today." I did the same with Aunt Mimi, Nate, Glenda and Burke, William, and Jill and told them to head home. They moved toward the exit while Nikki hung back.

"What's really going on?" she asked.

"Gage called the station and asked for someone to come and collect the trash. Roy came in with a to-go cup, and it disappeared. We need to know what was in that cup and if that's how he ingested something that caused him to get sick."

"Do you want Steve and me to hang around until you're ready to leave?"

I hugged my bestie. "No, you go do the newlywed thing, and we'll talk later, but if I could ask a tiny favor?"

She grinned. "No worries, Gage already mentioned the get-together tomorrow, and I'll make lasagna and dessert. Now, with the wrap-up tomorrow, we should still be able to play matchmaker for Sharon and EL."

I hugged her and said, "Thanks Nikki. I knew you'd jump in with your wand at the ready."

Gage and I watched our friends leave, and we were finally alone. "That was a good catch on your part. I never noticed

Roy brought anything with him. You might have helped catch the culprit and solved the case."

"We both know it's never that easy." I sat down in Roy's chair and settled in. Someone from the station would come quickly. I needed to clear my thoughts. I wish I had my chalkboard handy. It was my most used tool when trying to solve a puzzle, and Roy's near-death experience qualified. It wasn't like I could have one appear. It might lead to questions from Mac or Peabody, like how it got here. Feeling a little lost without it, I pulled up the notes feature on my cell. When I got home, I could transfer the details.

Gage sat close to me. "Tell me, why do you think this wasn't a simple accident?"

"Consider this. Chef Julian announced that the judges had allergies. Why would anyone judge a baking competition and take that chance? Especially since nuts and cinnamon are common ingredients in baking. If it were true about the cinnamon allergy, Roy is a self-proclaimed foodie. They usually enjoy almost every single thing that comes from the kitchen and are willing to try any kind of food. It's more logical that he's just not fond of the spice. It is the most common spice used not just in baking but main dishes, and there are even spice blends that use it. One example is apple pie spice. If he were truly allergic, he wouldn't have become a judge. There's too much room for variables."

"What about Blair and Julian? Do you think those allergies could be real? Blair said she carries an EpiPen with her. But when I needed one when Roy was suffering, she never volunteered it. Then, when I questioned her, she said it was missing. I thought it was very odd. If you have a life-threatening allergy, I would keep track of that since it would be my lifeline."

As fast as Gage was talking, I was tapping on the tiny

keyboard. "Blair's EpiPen was missing. Did she say when she had it last?"

"I'm assuming earlier today since she patted her jacket pocket and seemed genuinely distressed."

I cocked a brow. "Why?"

"The frantic patting of her pockets and the wide eyes."

"It's a single-dose medication." I paused and wondered how I would have reacted had I been in her shoes. "Being in the food business and eating out, she should carry a second one as a backup. At least I would."

The front door of the town hall groaned as it creaked open. "That must be the cavalry."

I couldn't help but smile. "Whoever it is won't think evidence sorting is part of the cavalry, but nice try."

Sharon and Mac sauntered in and took note of the now-empty room. We stood and pointed to the side of the room.

With a nod from Sharon, we moved to join them.

"Detective Erikson," Sharon said. "We have the van pulled up to the back so we can load up and get this back to the station. I have Jonesy on standby to help, too."

"Good. Now we're searching for a white to-go cup. It doesn't have a logo and based on the timeline, it should be near the bottom of the can. However, it might not have been tossed in this one, so we'll need to search through every trash can."

She gave an affirmative nod. "Ten-four."

"I'll run Lily back to her place and meet you at the station."

I pursed my lips. "I want to help. After all, it was my observation that led you in this direction."

"True, but this is all about evidence. If we need to use this to prosecute a criminal, chain of evidence is critical."

Knowing he was right was one thing, but not wanting to

miss out on the search was another. Then I had another thought. I could use the time they were sorting through trash to do some research on each judge. I stretched my arms over my head. "Okay. I would love to get into yoga pants and my old sweatshirt with a cup of hot tea anyway. It's been a long day."

Gage gave me an assessing look and leaned in close. For my ears alone, he said, "That was way too easy. What do you have up your sleeve other than your wand?"

I flashed him a sweet innocent smile. "Nothing for you to worry about. I'm just preparing for tomorrow." I stood on my tiptoes and kissed his cheek.

"Would you care to pinky promise on that?"

I thought it was funny that he wanted to fall back on our old childhood gesture. I held out my hand and crossed my fingers from my other hand behind my back. It might be immature, but after the day I had with all that baking, I needed a bit of childlike fun. "Of course, Sweetheart."

Chapter 6
Gage

I dropped Lily off at her place and jogged up the front steps and jerked open the heavy wooden door to the Town Hall. Mac was near the entrance and tossed me a pair of latex gloves. It was time to get down to the dirty job of sorting the trash for potential evidence.

"Did you get Lily home okay?" he asked.

"Yeah, and you and I know she'll be setting up her clue board."

He nodded. "She's got a mind for murder."

I gave him a sharp look. It wasn't murder, but it might have been, so I let that comment slide. "Have you found anything yet?"

"Nothing out of the ordinary. Peabody's checked the restrooms and is in the back room storage closet."

"Good." I pulled the gloves on and headed in the direction where I could hear her rustling about. "Detective, how's it going in there?"

"You need to take a look at this," Peabody's muffled voice drifted to us.

Mac held out a large, clear trash bag. "Take this."

I nodded and followed the sound of the detective's voice. I stepped inside the oversized closet. A single light bulb dimly lit the space. She had her police-issue flashlight trained to a back corner.

"What is it?"

"I don't know if it's relevant to our investigation, but this bin is filled with old, dried-up coffee cups. They look like they've been here a long time."

"Bag them. I've always followed the investigated path; if there is any possibility it might be related, we check it out." I understood Peabody's hesitancy. The dust around the rim of the trash can looked like it had been there for a decade. I pointed to the floor, "Run the light around this area."

She did as I asked. Kneeling on the floor, I hoped we finally had a tiny break. "Peabody, did you move the can when you came in?"

She shook her head. "I haven't touched anything in here. But I see what you mean. It looks as if it was moved recently." With a grin, she said, "I might have missed that fraction of an inch."

"I had a good mentor who helped me move from the cop's point of view to think more like a detective. When doing this job, the little things start to add up. Make sure you get some pictures of this area before you place the can into a trash bag."

"I should take the entire thing?" A crinkle creased her brow.

I was surprised at the question but she was a new detective. "Just a hunch, but someone may have touched the can, so there could be a useful print. It might be a long shot since it could have been jostled at any time but we should check it out."

She snapped open a bag before I could hand her the one

stuffed in my back pocket. Going forward, I knew she'd review the area with a keener eye. "I'm going back out front. If you need something else, just yell."

"Thanks, Detective."

I opened my mouth to ask her again to call me Gage but closed it. Taking on this job was a learning process right down to being comfortable calling me by my first name. When she was at dinner tomorrow night, I'd pull her aside and make the suggestion. At least when we were outside of working hours, we could be less formal. With a tip of my head in the direction of the door, I left.

Mac was directing a few uniform cops and making short work of it. It left me to go back behind the baking area. Had Lily and I overlooked a clue to what Roy Fletcher might have ingested? A slow smile crept over my face as I tapped out a text.

Any chance you took pictures of the baking area?

With a whoosh, it went through. I waited a moment before putting my phone back in my pocket on the off chance Lily would text me back. Even with the overhead lights, shadows filled the gaps between items on the shelves this late in the day. Since I didn't have my gear with me, the flashlight on my cell would have to do.

Everything reminded me of what I might see on the shelves of my mother's pantry except the white pastry boxes stuck on the corner shelf. There were several types of flour: pastry, whole wheat, almond, white, bread, rye, and even gluten-free. Then I looked at the sugar shelf. Brown, white, caster, confectionary, sanding, and something called turbinado. Then canisters of items I hadn't expected to see here: stevia, aspartame, and monk fruit.

I couldn't help but wonder which one would get used where, and if Lily knew about all these different types. I made a mental note to ask my mom if it became necessary to understand the difference. It was a good thing Lily had zero expectations for me to become a baker. I could cook regular meals and keep us fed. Our baked goods would come from the Sweet Spot and William.

My phone pinged with an incoming text. Lily.

Yes, and I'm printing them right now. My board is up and ready to review. XO

I wanted to ask if she had noticed anything specific yet, but that could wait until I was there in person. It would give Lily a chance to examine them. My reply was a thumbs-up.

I finished scanning the shelves. Nothing out of the ordinary jumped out at me. "Mac? Peabody?" They came from different directions of the building. "Are you headed back to the station now?"

"Yes, but it would be helpful if we knew more of what we were looking for? When do you think you'll hear from Mr. Fletcher's doctor?" Peabody asked.

"I'm going to head over to the hospital, and I'll swing by the station after. You should plan on quitting soon. There's no sense in working late until we know more." I snapped my fingers. "Don't forget, Lily said the cup was plain white. You can disregard anything else for now, but save everything. We may need to go back to it."

"I'll have the small trash can from the back dusted for fingerprints. Who knows what we might discover."

"Mac, will you lock up and let Lois know the building is secure?"

"Sure thing."

"If anything comes up, call me. Otherwise, I'll see you both tomorrow first here and then at Lily's for dinner."

Mac gave me a quizzical look.

Peabody said, "Lily wanted a bunch of us to get together for lasagna. I'll be there and EL is coming too."

A pink flush rose in her cheeks again. Mac quirked a brow in my direction.

"I'll check with Margaret when I get home. Is it okay if we bring Amanda?"

"Of course, as long as you don't mind the animals. Milo, my rescue Brutus, and Molly, Nikki's dog, will be there. It's a family affair."

"We've been thinking about adopting a dog. This would be a good chance to see how Amanda does being around both large and small animals."

"Fantastic. I'll let Lily know you're coming."

Mac chuckled. "I said I'd check with my bride, but you're right. I'm sure we'll be there."

Now that I felt I had a direction or at least a purpose, I was out the door. On my way to the hospital, I turned over the why's of Roy's collapse. If he knew he had an allergy, why didn't he have an EpiPen on him, too? What happened to Blair's? I only had her word that she even carried one. Every instinct I had was jabbing at me. This was a crime. If asked why I thought it wasn't just an accidental incident, I had nothing to go on. But I'd been around police work for a long time, and my instincts were rarely wrong. In my spare time, I devoured true crime books. I was all in until the culprit was caught, and I always used those as case studies on how to look at innocuous events that really were crimes. There was no such thing as a coincidence, only opportunity.

I turned on the radio and listened to the sports update on the short fifteen-minute drive into Pine Valley, to the county hospital. I was thankful to see that my truck was the only vehicle in the emergency room parking lot. That was a good indicator it had been a quiet afternoon for the ER team. I should be able to talk with the doctor and get back to Lily's within the hour, even with a quick stop at the station.

"Detective Erikson. It's good to see you again." The front desk clerk greeted me as I walked in. "How can I help you?"

"Hi, Mary. I wanted to check on Roy Fletcher, and I was hoping to speak with whichever doctor took care of him when Mr. Fletcher was brought in."

She pushed back from the desk. "Give me just a minute. I think Dr. Hammond is free."

As I waited, I studied the tropical fish tank in the waiting room. A few minutes later, I heard the door open behind me.

"Detective Erikson. I understand you have questions about Roy Fletcher." I withdrew my credentials and presented them so the doctor would know I was who I said.

I extended my hand to him. "Dr. Hammond?"

He smiled. "Yes."

We hadn't met before. He was short, maybe five feet six and lean and balding with ice blue eyes. Since he was new to the hospital, this was the first time we'd met, but I'd heard good things about him. "Gage Erikson. I'm a police detective from Pembroke Cove. I was hoping for an update on Roy Fletcher. We were told he had an allergy, and during the event today, I believe he went into anaphylactic shock."

He scanned my badge and shook my hand. "Good to meet you. At some point, I hope to get over to the police station and meet more of the officers in your department. I believe it's beneficial to have an open channel of communication. Not that I expect much to happen in this part of the country involving crime and medicine."

"Small Maine towns have their fair share of crime, Doctor. Don't let the bucolic setting fool you."

"Noted." He gave a brisk nod. "What specifically would you like to know about Mr. Fletcher?"

"We should start with what happened to him. Was it anaphylactic shock?"

He crossed his arms over his chest, his face expressionless. "Yes. He had an alert necklace in his pocket that states he's allergic to artificial sweeteners. The allergy is severe."

That was an interesting twist. "Don't you find it odd that he wasn't wearing it?"

The doctor nodded. "Yes. We noticed a rash on the back of his neck. I can't ask him, but I believe it's like when your watch is irritating and you take it off and put it in a pocket. If the EMT's had noticed it at the scene, it might have helped. However, there's no way to know for sure now."

"How is he now?"

This time Dr. Hammond's face drooped. "He's in a coma. Two things may have occurred: he ingested a great deal of the product, and he was slow to recognize his symptoms."

"I found it strange when we checked his jacket pockets and he didn't have an EpiPen."

Dr. Hammond's face grew thoughtful. "Which I too found odd. Rarely do I care for a patient with allergies who doesn't have one with them at all times. The old adage, better safe than sorry, is the golden rule when it comes to severe allergic reactions. It's a life-and-death kind of deal."

"How quickly would he have started to have symptoms after he consumed the sweetener?"

"It depends. The substance begins to be metabolized by the body anywhere from two, maybe as much as six hours."

That gave me something to noodle. Why would he have consumed anything artificial? And where was his emergency medicine? "How soon before I can talk to him?"

"It's hard to say. We're monitoring him closely, hoping to bring him out of the coma. Until that happens, we wait."

"In your professional opinion, how long might it take? For Roy to wake up?"

"The first twenty-four hours are critical. I hope we'll know more in the morning."

I shook his hand again and thanked him for his time. Handing him my card with my cell number, I said, "If anything changes in Mr. Fletcher's condition one way or the other, can someone let me know?"

He took my card and nodded. "Yes. I'll add this to his chart."

"One more question. Do you think it came from coffee? Could the taste have been disguised to where he wouldn't have noticed it?"

"It's possible. Some people can't tell the difference between real sugar and the fake stuff. Adding a lot of cream might have masked the flavor. It's hard to tell. Everyone's taste buds are different."

"Thanks again. I hope you have an uneventful night."

Dr. Howard said, "At least there's not a full moon. That helps."

I zipped my coat as I strode through the automatic ER doors and glanced at the crescent moon beginning to make its appearance. Thinking back to all the full moons that had occurred during patrol duty, I shuddered. Dr. Hammond was right. It brought out all kinds of crazy."

I had decided to skip the station and head right to Lily's. Her tidy bungalow with bright blue shutters would be my home once we were married, and I couldn't wait.

After talking with Dr. Howard, I concluded that Roy Fletcher's health emergency was a tragic accident. Wherever he had gotten coffee before coming to the baking contest, there must have been a mistake with his order. The only thing that still lingered was why he didn't have his EpiPen with him.

I continued to sit in my car until the chill penetrated the truck cab. The warm glow of the house seemed to welcome me. I wished I had thought to run home and grab Brutus, even though he had a doggie door for him to go out and do his business.

The curtains rustled, and a smile broke out over my face. Lily had picked up my oversized lap dog and he and Milo were sitting in the window, looking in my direction. I pushed open the truck door and jogged around the back side of the house. The door opened. Lily grabbed my hand and pulled me inside.

"I thought you'd never get here. How's Roy?" she asked.

"He's in a coma. But for your information, he was wearing a medical ID necklace that stated he's allergic to artificial sweeteners and not cinnamon."

A thoughtful look passed over her face. "Now that is interesting. Why did Chef Julian say otherwise?"

"Who knows, but we can ask him tomorrow." I kissed her soft lips and inhaled deeply. "Any chance we have dinner?"

She tipped her head and gave me a saucy grin. "I took a pan of macaroni and cheese from the freezer and tossed together a salad."

I patted my midsection. "Sounds good. When do we eat?"

"Later," she said, "you'll want to see what I've discovered first."

Chapter 7
Lily

I closed the door behind Gage and led the way into the living room. Milo was stretched out on the back of the sofa, and Brutus had taken up two of the three cushions. I gestured to the recliner and, with a flick of my wrist, turned it so that when Gage was sitting, he'd have a clear view of my clue board.

His brow shot to his hairline. "When did you learn how to move furniture?"

Milo grumbled, "Surprise. She's actually reading the book."

I popped my hands on my hips and glared at him. "For your information, my dear familiar, I've been much better about reading *Practical Beginnings* every day. I know I'm behind in learning spells and whatever else. You know, I might have more incentive to work harder if I knew when I might get a flying lesson or two."

Gage looked from me to Milo. Not that he could understand what my cat said but he'd get the gist of it based on my response.

"Now, you, my favorite witch and my favorite familiar should not be arguing."

Milo sat up and began kneading the back of the cushion with his claws. I cringed inwardly.

"You really need to remind Detective Cutie that I am not his familiar, so therefore, I can't be his favorite anything."

I wanted to stamp my feet and throw a mini temper tantrum. Milo needed to have a better understanding that once Gage lived with us after our wedding, I couldn't be pulled between the two of them. "We are a package, Milo. Deal with it."

Gage clasped my hand. "Did I upset the old man?"

Milo hissed. "Who's he calling old?"

I refused to acknowledge him and said to Gage, "He's fine. He's just hangry. Nothing more."

Milo jumped over Brutus and landed on the floor in front of the sofa. "Speaking of which, if you're choosing to delay dinner, I think it would be nice if you fed me and the oversized brute on the sofa."

I tapped the side of my leg, and Brutus, who wasn't a brute but a loveable Great Dane, followed me into the kitchen. Maybe if I fed them both, Milo would be in a better mood as I showed Gage the pictures I had taken from the baking event.

Gage trailed after us. "Does this mean we can eat and talk?"

I threw up my hands and sighed. No one was going to concentrate on the clues I discovered if they didn't have a full belly first. "Yes, we'll have dinner. Then we can get down to business."

With a wave of my hand, the table was set for two, complete with napkins, glasses, and plates. Gage took the casserole out of the oven, and I prepared the fur babies' plates next. The salad was in the refrigerator, so at least dinner was a quick set-up, and clean-up was literally a snap since I had perfected that spell.

I placed Milo's plate of cat food on the chair and Brutus's bowl on a platform. Milo had mentioned in passing that Brutus sometimes had neck pain. I talked with Nikki, and she suggested a stool.

Milo pushed his plate away and glared at me as his tail snapped up and down. "My dear witch, I think you've forgotten what my dinner should consist of unless you're trying to make me ill."

"What are you talking about? I gave you the fancy salmon dinner tonight." I picked it up and gave it a sniff to make sure it wasn't spoiled. "This is perfectly fine." I set it back down. Milo continued to assess me with his unrelenting eye contact. As if staring at me, he could take over my mind and make me bend to his will. Could he do that? He had been a very powerful witch in his day. I shifted my weight from one foot to the other as the contest of wills between witch and familiar waged on.

His voice was haughty, "It is not perfectly fine. Tonight, I would prefer a can of solid white albacore tuna packed in water as I maintain my sleek physique. As a side dish, a bit of smoked salmon with some curls of cheddar cheese on top."

I couldn't help the laughter that bubbled up from my toes and burst out. "I thought we had come to some sort of an agreement. Those *treats*," and I put extra emphasis on the word treat, "are for when you've done something amazing."

Milo stretched out on the chair and crossed his front paws one over the other. In his most annoyed voice, he said,

"I'm awesome all the time. However, I must point out how I've supported you in recent days. I haven't nagged you once about reading your book, *Practical Beginnings*. I've been totally supportive of your attempts to bake muffins and such that will be edible. And," he jabbed his paw in my direction, "I haven't once asked for a special treat. Combine all those together, I'd say I'm overdue for some TLC."

By this time, I had covered my mouth to smother my laughter as my entire body shook. "Milo. You're kidding."

He turned his head to the side. "Where would you be without me? I've always believed in you. That should be worth something."

Gage leaned against the counter, listening to this one-sided conversation. "I'm taking a leap. Milo isn't happy with his dinner."

"Nope, he wants tuna, smoked salmon, and cheddar cheese instead."

He shrugged. "Why not give it to him?"

Milo's head snapped up. "See. Detective Cutie agrees with me, sweet."

Knowing I was on the losing end of this conversation, it was time to strike a deal. "If I agree to give in to your request, you will eat normal kitty food for the next week unless, of course, you do something extraordinary."

"Um, I think you need to clarify since I do something amazing every day. After all, I'm your familiar, so guiding you in the ways of all things witch takes an enormous amount of intelligence and patience."

I threw up my hands. "I find you maddening. How about you come up with a compromise since you are not going to have smoked salmon, cheese, and tuna every day."

He rose to a sitting position and remained quiet for several long seconds. The kitchen clock ticked as I waited.

"I've got it!" he announced. His excitement rolled off his little gray fur in waves.

"I'm listening."

"If you permit me to indulge tonight, I will only request special meals if I've saved you from certain death, encouraged you to read the book and successfully learn a spell, or come up with the clue that solves the crime or generally helps you in any way." If a cat could have a smug smile, Milo would be wearing one. "What do you think? Does it sound agreeable?"

I pulled out a chair and sat down so that I could look him in the eye at his level. "Basically, what you've described is your special meal can be requested for any reason if you can justify it."

"My dear witch, I adore you and your quick mind. Just say yes. Your future husband is going to perish before he has an opportunity to enjoy that delicious meal you've defrosted, and we don't want him to become a ghost."

"Lily, why not just give him the dinner he'll enjoy? I think you're putting too much into this test of wills. Milo is a part of your, no, our family, and we want the best for each other. What harm will it do?"

I pushed back the chair and picked up Milo's plate with the now-congealed cat food. "Fine I'm doing this, but, Milo?"

He tipped his head. His eyes were round orbs of deep green. "Yes?"

"You'll tone down some of your snark when it comes to me reading my book, and we will schedule flying lessons."

"You can't have flying lessons until you attend coven meetings. That's in the book, and if you had—"

I held up my hand. "I know, read the book, I'd be in the loop."

Gage chuckled. "Oh, living with the two of you is going to be highly entertaining."

With a snap of my fingers, the canned cat food was gone. In its place was all the requested items. Jabbing a finger in my familiar's direction I said, "I'll go to the next coven meeting, and you're going with me." I set the plate in front of Milo.

"This looks delicious, and of course, I will accompany you. If I didn't, I would be reprimanded for abandoning my witch. That is one infraction a familiar never wants to be accused of." Milo stopped talking and delicately picked up a small chunk of tuna, effectively blocking everything out but his dinner.

Gage crossed the room and wrapped me in a hug. "I'm starving, but first, I would like to kiss my lady." He nibbled my neck as his lips created a trail of little kisses to mine.

I pushed my quarrel with Milo away and was reminded how much this man loved me and I him.

With the kitchen cleaned up and a dog, familiar, man, and witch full from a wonderful meal, I was now in the living room, standing in front of my chalkboard. We had mugs of a chamomile tea blend my mom had just made. Gage was on the sofa waiting for me to show him what I had discovered.

I picked up my wand. Gage pulled back into the cushions.

"Are you about to spell the pictures?"

"No. I don't want them to come to life or anything wacky like that. I'm using it as a pointer." You'd think growing up with a mother as a witch, he'd be less nervous around me and my wand.

I shrugged a shoulder. "Don't worry, it's not like a

loaded gun. I have to say something with an intention for a spell actually to be cast."

He relaxed. "I know that."

Milo looked up from his spot on the back of the sofa and said, "Yeah. Right. DC thinks you're like a gunslinger in the Wild West."

I didn't bother to respond to the abbreviation of Gage's nickname or the gunslinger comment but focused on the board. "You haven't told me yet what you found out at the hospital."

"I'm sorry, Lily. I got distracted with dinner and Milo. It got pushed to the back burner, so to speak." He sat up straight. "I spoke with the doctor who treated Roy when he was brought into the emergency room. We were right about the allergic reaction; cinnamon didn't cause the attack. Apparently, Roy had a medical alert necklace in his pocket, and it lists he's allergic to artificial sweeteners. But I didn't find it when I looked for an EpiPen."

"That's interesting. But why wouldn't he have emergency medicine like an EpiPen?" I chewed the inside of my cheek. "At least it supports what Chef Julian said; Roy isn't allergic to the spice. But why would anyone cook with artificial anything in a baking contest unless it was a requirement? Everyone knows it can leave an aftertaste or change the flavor of a baked good."

"I'm not sure, but this might change what you found in the supply area."

I picked the first image off the board and tucked the tape over the edge. "This is of the spice area. You can see here I circled the Chinese Five Spice. It's irrelevant now."

"Why?" Gage held out his hand, and I passed it to him.

"I saw Dora add this to her Leftover Cranberry Muffin recipe. I didn't think anything about it at the time. After I got home I researched all the ingredients that I wasn't familiar with. I was surprised to learn cinnamon is one of the five spices used. I thought for sure this was the reason Roy collapsed."

"We should be looking at the sweetener section." He handed the photo back to me.

I took another image after scanning the lot of them. "Take a look at this. There are several types of fake sugar on the shelf. But the jars look full. Did the doctor say how long or how much he would have ingested to have such a deadly effect on Roy?"

"A couple of hours for it to work. There's no way to tell how much he might have consumed. Until he wakes up, we can't ask him the questions that would help us figure out if he was targeted or if it was just an unfortunate accident. Peabody and Mac pulled all the garbage from the town hall. She made a curious discovery." He picked up his mug of tea and sipped it.

I waved my hand to get him to hurry up and tell me. "What did Sharon find?"

"In the back room, there was a garbage can. It was filled with white to-go coffee cups. They appeared to be old, as there was dust around the rim of the garbage can. But the interesting part is it had recently been moved. There was a ring of dust on the floor where it had been. Now, obviously, it could have gotten moved at any point or for any reason."

"But maybe, if someone had wanted to hurt Roy, they tossed his cup in there, and we'll find proof." I tapped my lip with the tip of my wand. "Roy comes to the event. Someone gives him a cup of tainted coffee. He drinks it and, over the next hour or so, starts to have symptoms; maybe he's perplexed and ignores them. After all, wouldn't he know if he had eaten something that would cause a reaction? When it gets to the point of no return, he falls off his chair, and the rest is history."

Gage was nodding as I spoke. "It's a solid working theory, but why would anyone want to harm Roy? Blair and Julian seemed to like and respect him."

"Maybe one of the contestants had a grudge against him. Daisy told me the judges go from contest to contest, just like the bakers. He could have made an enemy somewhere along the way."

I withdrew a piece of chalk from my pocket. In the middle of the board, I wrote Roy Fletcher and circled his name. A prickle of excitement raced down my spine. This is what I had been itching to do for months since the death of Petra Addington. Putting the clues down and working the puzzle always gave me a thrill, and I usually helped Gage put the bad guy or gal away, too.

"Lily, the man didn't die. He's in a coma."

I put my hand on one hip and gave him a side-eye. "Tell me you don't think this is a crime, and I'll stop writing."

He pointed to the board. "Keep going."

I jotted down the names of the nine contestants including Blair and Julian and *Missing EpiPen*. It was a start.

Chapter 8
Lily

The next morning, I wandered into the living room. The weak rays of the early morning sun were inching across the floor. I wanted to take another look at my clue board. Gage and I hadn't gotten much further than jotting down a list of everyone who might have a slight reason for hurting Roy. But without knowing if anyone had threatened him recently, what could be the real motive? Roy and Julian's friendship? Blair couldn't be holding that against Roy. Were baking competitions so fierce that someone would want revenge on a judge? That theory might hold more substance, but not by much. Could someone else have wanted to be a part of the judges' table and was excluded for some unknown reason?" I added XX and a question mark as another line back to Roy's name in the center of the board.

What was I missing? Milo serpentined around my legs. "Any thoughts of breakfast cross your mind, Lily?" He rubbed his head against my foot as he rolled over belly up. "You should have a big breakfast: eggs, ham, maybe home fries, and a scone too. Of course, copious amounts of coffee.

I happen to know for a fact you didn't sleep well last night. All that tossing and turning robbed me of my beauty sleep."

I scooped Milo up and rubbed the downy, soft fur between his ears. "I'm sorry, fur baby. It's just I can't get this Roy thing off my mind. He seems likable to the contestants and other judges; even Nancy seems to like him. Do you think it was an accident?"

He tipped his head and placed a paw, sans claws, on my cheek. "Do you? That's the more important question here. Trust your instincts. That's one of the traits you must work on as a witch. Questioning yourself in any situation could have dire consequences."

"It's hard to be sure, but a man severely allergic to something like artificial sweeteners wouldn't take any chances. If he had known it was in his coffee, there's no way he would have drunk a drop. This was not accidental." I gave a brisk nod of my head, kissed Milo, and placed him on the floor. "No time to cook a real breakfast."

"You're a witch. With a quick spell, you could have breakfast fit for a queen or king, in my case, familiar."

I had been wanting to try a new spell I found in my book. I grinned. "Okay, but if the spell goes wrong, there's no poking fun at the effort, and you have to eat what I spell up."

He contemplated my terms for about ten seconds before he agreed. "You should do the spell in the kitchen. It's an enclosed space, so if something goes wrong, there will be less mess."

My shoulders sagged. "What kind of witch do you think I am?"

He sauntered into the kitchen and hopped up on the counter next to the sink. "We're still defining your role, unlike Nikki, who's a kitchen witch, or Mimi, who's a cosmic witch. You have much potential, but refining it is taking longer than I thought."

"I'm not sure to take that as a compliment or a complaint." I summoned my wand from my tote bag. If a cat could beam with pride, that would be the description I'd have given for Milo's face and body language as he watched me.

I thought about what spell I should cast. "*My familiar and me are hungry. I wish for eggs, bacon, bread, and hot coffee. This I wish so it shall be.*" It wasn't the most creative, but at least it sort of rhymed. I blinked and my mouth fell open. On the counter was a slab of bacon, a hen laying an egg, a sack of flour, and a mug of steaming coffee.

"Milo, what did I do wrong? This should be cooked and ready to eat."

My familiar actually sniggered at me. "You never specified that the items should be prepared except for the coffee. It wasn't a bad spell. It'll need refinement for the next time."

With a flick of my wrist, the ingredients vanished while the coffee remained. A tap on the back door proceeded before it opened. Nikki stepped inside.

"Good morning. I knew you'd be up early and thought you'd like a good breakfast before we head back to the contest."

Milo sat up straighter. "Does that include four-legged coven members, too?"

She stroked the front of his chest. "Of course. I'd never forget about you." She placed a woven basket on the now-cleared counter. As she unpacked scones, cream, fruit salad, and a bowl of eggs, she said, "I was hoping to hear what you and Gage came up with last night about our new case."

I quirked a brow. "*Our* new case?"

"Yup. I didn't want to call last night, but when Steve

and I were leaving, I overheard Daisy and Geoff talking. Apparently, Julian and Blair have a long-running love-hate relationship. Which got me thinking. What if Roy wasn't the intended victim?"

"Blair is allergic to peanuts and Julian, almond flour." I magicked a frying pan onto the stove and then retrieved plates and silverware from the sideboard. My contribution was setting the table.

"After talking things over with Milo, I'm making an assumption that Roy wasn't the intended target, even though it was aspartame that caused him to collapse. It would make sense about Julian or Blair. We need to ask questions after we get to town hall today."

"Then we'll most certainly need full stomachs to plan our sleuthing." Nikki pointed to the kitchen chair. "Have a seat and we'll make a plan." She tapped her brow. "Ms. Holmes, your personal Doctor Watson is ready and willing to assist."

I couldn't help but smile. This had become a running joke between us, Gage, and Steve that I was Holmes and Nikki was my Watson.

Moments later, two plates overflowing with eggs, sliced fruit, scones, and crisp bacon were on the table, one for me and one for Milo.

Licking his lips, he said, "Now, this is breakfast. Lily, take note of the smoked salmon in my eggs. Nikki knows how to cook up a veritable feast for this handsome familiar."

I groaned, but a smile graced my mouth. Not only was Nikki good to Milo, but I also had a dollop of whipped cream on my fruit. "Between this and baking, I'm going to gain ten pounds." I gave her a wink. "Maybe I should take up jogging."

She pulled out the chair and placed her plate on the

table as she chuckled. "That's a statement I haven't heard in a few months. Besides, why start now? The holidays are upon us, and with all the cookie trays that will be dropped at stores and events, you might as well indulge. After the new year, we'll start exercising. You have a big day next year, and exercise is a great stress reducer."

I knew what she was referring to, and I was also considering a June wedding to Gage. There was something old-fashioned about being a June bride. It was only fair that I talk with him first, but Nikki would be at the top of the list when we finally set our date.

I picked up my fork. "Breakfast first, and then we'll get our sleuth on."

Nikki and I got to the town hall mid-morning just as the doors were unlocked. We strolled in, and to anyone looking, we were all casual like and just early for the event. Julian and Blair were at the judge's table. I jabbed Nikki in the side and inclined my head in the general direction.

I dropped my voice so it wouldn't carry across the room. "What do you think, the direct approach to see how Roy is and then slide into the topic of allergies?"

"I'll follow your lead."

We wove through the chairs, and I made sure my smile was friendly. "Good morning. Chef Julian, Blair. Have you heard anything about Roy Fletcher's condition?"

"Good morning, ladies." He flashed us that oh-so-slick, insincere smile that he'd been doing yesterday. I doubted he even knew what the word meant. "Blair and I stopped at the hospital last night, but we couldn't visit him. It's just tragic, a reaction to aspartame. He's comatose. The doctor isn't sure if he'll wake up. Ever."

I took a step back. If I had been delivering that kind of news, I wouldn't have a glib tone in my voice. Blair's mouth turned down at the corners, but the sorrow barely reached her eyes. Neither of these people knew how to fake empathy.

"Hopefully, we'll hear good news today. I want to reassure to the final bakers Roy will be fine." He rubbed his hands together. What was it with this annoying habit of his? "I'll bet you're excited to be in the finals. We know you had a slight hiccup with your oven, but you had a brilliant concept, and Fred Wickshire thought you deserved to move on. Of course, Blair and I agreed. I'm a huge fan of any kind of biscotti."

That explained how I made it through to the final round. Biscotti and Fred. "It should be a fun time. I'm not sure I'm at the same level of expertise as the others in the competition."

Blair picked up a to-go coffee cup and sipped. "Nonsense. Everyone starts at the same spot—even Julian and myself, although we were much younger when we met in culinary school." She laughed and poked his arm. "Do you remember? That's when we actually liked each other."

"I had no idea you went way back?" Nikki said.

Julian nodded, "Before I became a best-selling cookbook author and Blair opened her bakeries."

"Best-selling with my recipes." She glared at him and rolled her eyes but addressed Nikki and me. "Do you want to know the unvarnished truth?"

She tossed the long locks of her auburn hair over her shoulder in a dismissive act while his nostrils flared. "Even in school, Julian would borrow a recipe and pass it off as his own. But he could never execute it in the kitchen. Back then, I didn't care as much; I knew I was a talented baker. It was only when my bakery chain exploded that he broke into my flagship store in Boston and stole my best recipes. Then he had the audacity to publish them as his own."

Julian's neck began to turn red. I had witnessed this yesterday. That expression hot under the collar was coined just for him. "Blair. I was entitled to those recipes. We developed them together in school. They were as much my intellectual property as yours."

"We're not going down this road again, Julian. But to refresh your addled memory. Wasn't it enough that you've made a fortune off writing a few cookbooks that you had to try to destroy me by putting dead rats in the Portland store? Come on, that was low even for you."

"I've said you needed to prove that allegation. Which you can't because it wasn't me."

This conversation was spinning in a direction that wasn't helpful. I needed to know about the allergies of everyone involved.

I held up my hands in an attempt to divert their attention. "Maybe this isn't the best place to bring up the topic of who did what to whom and when. After all, poor Roy is lying in a hospital bed."

Julian stuffed his hands into his black and white checked chef pants. "Lily's right. We need to stop bickering and focus on today."

Blair tipped her cup and frowned. "I need more coffee."

Nikki held out her hand. "I'll get it for you."

She tipped her head. "Why, thank you. I'd like a fresh cup. A healthy pour of cream and two packets of the pink stuff."

"Julian, would you like a cup too?"

"Yes, just cream."

Blair's coffee sounded like something that Roy might

have drank. "Do you know how Roy took his coffee? I noticed he was enjoying a cup when I got here yesterday." My shoulders slumped, knowing that sounded lame.

Julian's mouth pursed to one side. "That's an odd question."

"Sometimes I ask off-beat questions." I paused, waiting for one of them to answer. Gage was terrific with the question and pause method until a suspect couldn't stand it anymore and spilled the beans, or, in this case, coffee beans.

"He doesn't use sugar or sweetener of any kind, with a large splash of cream. I swear it looks more tinged cream than it does coffee. But to each their own." Blair shrugged her shoulders and sat down in the chair she had occupied yesterday. "Do you think his coffee had something to do with getting sick?"

Julian glanced around the empty room, leaned in closer to me, and lowered his voice as he spoke. "I'll share a little secret with you. Neither Roy nor I have allergies to cinnamon like I insinuated, but Blair can't even touch nuts, or she gets deathly ill. It's one of the hallmarks of her bakeries. Everything she bakes is free from nuts."

"What about the almond flour? Would that be an issue for either of you?"

Blair said, "Yes. Julian told the truth about that even though he said he didn't like the texture. It's mild compared to what happened to Roy. Having a reaction to the sweetener like that. Julian gets hives when he eats anything with almond flour."

"Julian, your allergy is mild?"

He lifted a shoulder. "Annoyance is a better description."

Nikki came back and handed each of them a cup of coffee. "Here you go."

People began to filter into the room, and I said, "I'd better get ready. We should be starting soon."

Julian shook my hand, "Good luck today."

Blair gave me a pointed look, "Rumor has it Lily has some award-winning recipes at her disposal."

I thought back to when I checked in yesterday and Nancy said she couldn't be a judge because she had given me her pie recipe. But how Blair had just spoken to me? Had I done something unethical?

Nikki looped her arm through mine. "Don't pay any attention to her. The recipe doesn't make the baker."

I dug through my shoulder bag. Dang it, I left my laminated cards at home. My mouth went dry. There was no way I could do anything without those. "Nikki, I forgot my recipes. What am I going to do?"

She winked, put her hand in her jacket pocket, and withdrew my cards. "You might not be able to do magic, but I can."

I exhaled. Relief was like a warm, calming wave washing over me. "Thank you. Now to see if I can remember all that you taught me and at least be able to finish what I've started."

Chapter 9
Gage

The town hall was standing room only when I arrived for the baking contest. I stopped at the hospital on the way. I wasn't sure if I wanted to share with Lily what I'd learned about Roy Fletcher's condition. Seeing Lily smiling and chatting with contestants with Nikki by her side was oil on the troubled waters of my thoughts. As if she could feel me watching her, she lifted her hand and smiled. Even from this distance, I could see the sparkle in her eyes, or was it I knew her so well that I had come to count on it?

Walking down the center aisle and turning right, I made my way to her. As I drew closer, she searched my face, and her smile dimmed. I wrapped my arms around her and held her tight. She waited until my hug loosened and looked at me.

"What happened? It's Roy." That didn't have to be a question. She just knew and cut right to the heart of the situation.

I nodded and clasped her hand in mine, drawing her in the direction I had come.

We stepped outside into the frosty air and crossed the wide stone steps. Lily hugged her arms around her body as she shivered. I slipped off my down jacket and wrapped it her around her shoulders.

"Thank you." With a glance around us, she cleared her throat. "Are you ready to tell me what's happened?"

We were the only people outside. It seemed anyone who was coming to the bake-off was already indoors. "I swung by the hospital before coming into town. You know to check on Roy."

Her hand flew to cover her gaping mouth. "Oh no."

"He's still alive. But someone snuck into his room late last night and tried to smother him with a pillow. Luckily, the nurse was coming in to check his vitals and stopped the assailant in the act."

Her face drained of color. "And, and, he's going to be okay?" My sweet witch was born with an empathy streak as wide as the Atlantic Ocean.

"Yes. I spoke with Dr. Hammond, and Roy is reacting to more stimulation. In time, they hope he'll make a full recovery as long as there are no other complications."

She chewed the bottom corner of her lip, and the wrinkle between her pretty, sable, brown eyes deepened. "Nikki and I came over early. We were hoping to see if we could learn something from Julian and Blair."

I didn't like where this was going. Once again, Lily might have unwittingly put a target on her back, not to mention Nikki. However, I had to give her credit. She hadn't come down here alone to ask questions, and between the two women, their magic was extremely powerful, especially if dealing with non-magical people. "You've got my full attention. What did you learn?"

"Julian and Blair went to see Roy at the hospital last night, but they said they weren't permitted in. Is it possible they hung around, and one of them tried to prevent him from waking up?"

Rubbing my hand over my chin I said, "At this point anything is possible. We don't have a motive. All we have are suspects. From the two most obvious, Chef Julian and Blair, to the contestants. Who knows, maybe even Nancy was somehow involved."

Lily snapped her fingers. "She offered me a coffee or tea yesterday and mentioned she had gotten one for Roy." She clutched my arm and pressed her fingertips into my skin. "She has to be on the list. Even if I think it's impossible. She's been nice and helpful with me getting ready for the contest."

I understood exactly what Lily meant. However, I wasn't about to point out that we had several people who we thought were harmless do some very bad things, including almost taking the life of my beautiful fiancée. "On the positive side, we know this wasn't an accident. I'll dig more into Roy's background. Keep your ears open. Somebody might mention that he was arguing with someone before we arrived yesterday. People always see things they don't realize was important."

Lily glanced at the main doors. "I'll talk to Nancy. I've known her a long time. She might be more comfortable chatting with me than you or even Sharon."

I cupped her rosy cheek with my now chilled hand. "Please don't go anywhere alone with anyone. That includes Nancy. Until we can get this sorted out, everyone is a suspect."

"Is it okay that I fill Nikki in too? I wouldn't want her getting into a tight spot either."

"Of course, and it goes without saying, ask her to keep this confidential. I don't want to spook anyone."

I slipped my arm around her shoulders and pulled her close to me, kissing her temple and inhaling the subtle fragrance of vanilla. "You're going to do great in there today."

She tipped her head back and looked into my eyes. Hers were like smooth milk chocolate. "I just want to produce something edible and without causing a fire or other ruckus."

I tweaked her nose. "You? Create a ruckus? It's not possible."

We both laughed since there were occasions where mischief and mayhem had followed her.

The large wooden door opened. Nikki stepped out, first looking to her right and then left. "Hey, you two. Stop playing kissy face and come inside. It's almost time for Chef Julian to announce the next challenge."

With a saucy wink she said, "My whisk awaits."

I held Lily close for another moment, not quite ready to let her go. I'd never been one to follow a niggling feeling. It usually had to be a strong gut reaction. Today, I just couldn't relax with her participation in the contest. The only comfort I had was that in a split second, she could cast a protection spell around herself and anyone else she thought needed it.

Chef Julian stood on the stool. "Bakers, in just a moment, the contest will get underway. Today, you will bake two items as we had a nonelimination round yesterday. Each baker is instructed to create a cupcake using cranberries as the main element." He looked at his watch. "You have five minutes to gather your thoughts."

I was glad they hadn't asked me for ideas since the only combination I could think of was cranberry and orange. It was not original in the least. Lily had been practicing cupcakes. I wasn't sure how hers would compare against the others. She had one thing going for her— she was very creative. Thinking outside the box was how she had solved many types of puzzles, including a few murders that had occurred in town.

Julian clanged an oversized spatula against an empty pitcher. "Bakers. Begin."

Twenty minutes elapsed. The audience was focused on what the contestants were whipping up. I glanced over my shoulder Nikki was standing against the wall. Her hand movements were like she was the one whisking ingredients together. I stood up and excused myself as I walked in front of the row of spectators, including my folks and Lily's family.

In a horse whisper I asked, "Nik, what are you doing?"

"I'm so nervous I couldn't sit still another minute. Cupcakes might sound easy, but to bake a super moist cake and balance it with perfect buttercream is hard. Toss in cranberries, which are a difficult flavor to combine with others, would be challenging for an experienced baker."

I dropped my voice and glanced in the direction of the contestants. Lily was looking at the batter. Her face blank. Had Nikki been somehow helping her? "Are you?" I flicked my wrist like I was holding a wand like the fictional witches do in the movies.

She thrust her chin out, and her eyes narrowed to mere

slits. "Gage. My stars. What kind of witch do you think I am?"

"I'm sorry. But I see you over here like your baking, which mimics Lily's movements. We start talking, and she stares at the cupcake tin."

"Lily would never ask for that kind of help. I'm dealing with nervous energy. When I feel like my insides are flipping out, I bake. It calms me. Since I'm not leaving Lily, it was easier to step away and pretend." In a carefully controlled tone, she asked, "Don't you think Lily's capable of doing this on her own?"

From the corner of my eye, I saw Lily sliding the tin into the oven and setting an old-style rotary dial timer. It was one I recognized. In spite of irking Nikki, I loved that Lily had incorporated my mom's kitchen timer into the contest.

"Please don't tell her that I had a moment where I didn't believe in her ability. I'm having a very strange day. I can't shake an uneasy feeling."

"How long has this been going on?"

I had Nikki's full attention. She knew me almost as well as Lily did. Over the years, I had come to think of her more like a sister as well as my girl's best friend. "Ever since I arrived. I'm not sure if Lily shared with you, but someone tried to kill Roy Fletcher last night. Even though in the beginning, we thought what happened was an accident. No one would attempt murder if that had been the reality."

She placed a gentle hand on my shoulder. "I get it. Intuition is not part of my gifts; however, I've felt an oppressiveness since coming inside, too."

"What do we do?" Now that I knew she felt it, I relaxed a little. With her magical prowess and my skills as a detective, we could handle any situation, right?

She bobbed her head in Lily and the contestants' direction. "We wait, keep our eyes open, and be ready for anything."

I crossed my arms over my chest and planted my feet shoulder-width apart. If anyone was thinking of any funny business, I hoped my presence, along with that of Peabody and Mac, would be a deterrent.

Chef Julian rose from his chair and bestowed a benevolent smile on the audience. "I don't know about all of you, but the aromas emanating from those ovens are most certainly setting my taste buds into overdrive."

Nods rippled through the crowd, and a low murmur of excitement followed. Julian clasped his hands behind his back and strolled behind the bakers, looking over shoulders and perusing their clipboards.

"What do you think he's doing?"

Nikki leaned in and whispered. "Showing off."

I clapped my hand over my mouth to stifle a laugh. Lily looked over; her brows furrowed together, and she mouthed, *What mischief are you two plotting?*

I shrugged in response and grinned.

Crash!

The sound came from the entrance. Peabody and Mac were already in motion. Chef Julian jumped up. In a loud voice he said, "People, remain in your seats."

I was almost to the door when it opened. Mac looked inside and stopped when he saw me. "Detective, will you step outside? There's something you need to see."

I closed the door behind me and crossed the wide steps to where Peabody was holding what looked like a metal street sign. "What's that?"

She held up the sign that stated MOOSE CROSSING. "Detective, I think it was propped against the door, but look at the backside." She turned it over.

In red spray paint, it said *Revenge Proves Its Own Executioner*.

Mac said, "By the time we got out here, the street was quiet just like it is now, so no hope of a witness."

What did this have to do with the contest? "You didn't find anything else?"

The detectives shook their heads. Peabody said, "Just the sign. By the looks of the reverse side, it seems like it had rusted off the post."

I looked closer. Peabody was correct. The rusty metal fragments remained where the pole should have been; it wasn't vandalized and just utilized for the message board.

The door eased open, and Lily poked her head around it. "Everything okay out here?"

"Nothing serious." I moved to block her view of the sign, hoping she wouldn't venture out. After all, she was in the midst of a competition. That thought was short-lived as she caught sight of Peabody holding the sign.

"Sharon, what's that?"

At this moment, it wouldn't do any good to attempt to redirect her back inside. I moved aside for her to walk past me.

Peabody tipped the sign so Lily had a clear view of the front and back. A hint of a smile teased at the corner of her lips as she read *moose crossing* out loud. But that vanished as she saw the opposite side.

Lily frowned. "That's a famous quote by John Ford." She rubbed her hand over her chin. She read it again. "Gage, is it possible this has anything to do with Roy Fletcher's attempted murder?"

Lily had cut to the core of the questions already forming in my mind. "It's possible. We still don't know why anyone would want to hurt him, let alone try and finish the job his allergy attack didn't."

She gave me a pointed look. "You need to find a way to keep Julian and Blair in town. And check the people who are gathered here. Anyone who's not a resident should be noted."

An image of Lily in a police uniform crossed my mind. She would have made a great cop.

"Sweetheart. Peabody and Mac are here. As soon as possible, they're going to take Julian and Blair in for questioning about the attempt on Roy's life. I don't want to disturb the contest and put the guilty party on alert. As far as people attending today, Jonesy's at the door, and everyone who came in was cross-referenced with attendees yesterday. We have a complete list."

Lily nodded when I mentioned Officer Jones. He was solid, and I trusted him to be thorough.

She tapped the corner of the sign. "Gage, somebody is sending a warning. The unknown was the message directed to someone inside, but more important, why?"

Chapter 10
Lily

I hurried back inside. Shivering. The cold air gave me a chill after spending the last half hour in front of an oven. My mind was in overdrive after seeing the sign with that message in red paint. The last thing I wanted to do was try to bake something. I skirted around the chairs on the right side of the room to get back to my baking station. Each step felt like my shoes were covered with wet but fast-drying cement.

There were so many unknowns in what had become the case of Roy Fletcher. Could his life be protected long enough until we found the responsible party or parties? I locked eyes on Julian as he sat with his arms crossed over his pristine white chef coat. What did I really know about this man who proclaimed to be an award-winning author? However, if what Blair said was accurate, he stole her recipes, and heaven only knew what else to publish the book.

I pumped a generous dollop of soap into my hands and washed them well under steaming water as I studied the people in front of me. Some were chatting to their neighbors, others focused on their cell phones, and even one or two seemed to be napping. I guessed watching a baking competition could be like watching a pot boil. The best part was when there were samples available to savor.

The interesting pair that held my attention were Blair and Julian. Their heads were together, and their facial expressions were dour. Blair was lightly pounding her fist into her opposite hand. Julian shook his head and placed his over hers. I could read his lips. He kept saying no, paused, and said no two more times.

Blair wrenched her hand from his and pushed back from the table brushing past Nancy as she got up from her chair. They headed for the coffee station and with their backs to me. I had no idea what the women were talking about.

Observing from a distance was like watching a movie without the sound. I could only guess what was going on. I could cast a spell to hear them, but I had dedicated the time at the town hall to be witchcraft-free. I would keep my word to myself. After all, what kind of a witch would I be if I couldn't refrain from using my magic? I had spent years not even knowing I was one. It was time I refreshed my old skill set.

"Lily. Your timer went off on your cupcakes."

I flashed Daisy a grateful smile. "Thanks. I don't know what I'd have done without you during this contest. Between yesterday letting me know my oven wasn't working and today keeping my little cakes from getting over-cooked. One word. Lifesaver."

"Think nothing of it. I've enjoyed having a newbie at this event. You're not taking anything overly serious, which is refreshing." She methodically placed her cupcakes on the wire rack and smiled to herself.

. . .

Why would Daisy say I wasn't serious about my cupcakes or anything I had made so far? Just entering the contest indicated I was serious about being a part of this event. I dried my hands and found the cake tester buried under a few other tools. Once I confirmed my cupcakes were done, I mimicked Daisy's actions and set them on a rack to cool. But first, I wanted to take them out of the silicone liners so that they'd cool faster. Juggling the hot cupcake in my hands, I pushed on the bottom, silently wishing for heat-proof fingertips. When it popped out, part of the cake was still in the liner.

I could feel sweat beads pop above my lip, my breaths came in quicker gasps. What had I done wrong? Looking in the direction of where Nikki had been sitting, her chair was empty. I scanned the room and saw her standing in the aisle.

I exhaled with relief. But how could she help me?

She held up her two hands and pushed them in a downward motion like I needed to slow down. Then she held up her third and then fourth fingers. Finally, it dawned on me. I needed to take a few minutes before I popped the cakes out.

While I waited, my thoughts turned to Blair. When I didn't see her back in her chair, I slipped behind the bakers. Maybe now was a good time to get a mug of tea for myself. If anyone asked, I needed it to soothe my frazzled nerves. Not that I was nervous, well, much. I had made it to day two.

Nancy gave me a tight smile. "Lily. Can I get something for you?" She gestured to the table that was loaded with coffee and tea supplies.

"No, thank you, Nancy. I can fix a cup of tea."

She followed me, which reminded me of how she had followed Blair just a short time ago.

"How are you feeling about your chances today?" She handed me an empty cup. I dropped the tea bag in and gave her a quick side-eye. "Like yesterday. I'm doing my best, but I'm not in the same league as these pro-amateur bakers."

"Nonsense. You've been mentored by some of the best cooks in the county, William and Nikki, along with your aunt. I would have loved to have learned from such experienced bakers. My mother was an excellent cook, but she always said baking was far too precise for her. She even bought our birthday cakes from the grocery store." She cast a wistful eye in Julian's direction and quickly looked away. "I'm capable enough. If only I'd finished culinary school, I would be great."

Confidence didn't roll off her. But looking at Julian and talking about school prompted a new line of questions. "Nancy, I had no idea you were training to be a chef?"

A shy smile appeared on the other woman's face while her gaze darted around the room. "I wanted to be a pastry chef. All of the chefs I was training under said I showed great promise with my ability to blend flavors. In fact, the pie recipe that I shared with you was one of the most highly rated."

"What school did you attend?" Was it possible she knew more about Julian and Blair than she'd let on?

She glanced in the judges' direction before she averted her eyes and studied the floor. "The culinary institute in downstate New York." She straightened the pile of paper napkins on the table. "Oh dear, we're almost out of supplies." She hurried away before I could say anything else and closed the closet door behind her with a firm click.

I finished fixing my cup of tea and made the way to my

station via Gage. If he was surprised to see me, he never changed his happy expression.

I bent over his chair and leaned in close so others wouldn't hear me. "Can you check something out?"

His brow quirked. "You've learned something?"

"Nancy attended the same culinary school as our judges. The interesting twist is that she didn't finish. The way she looked at Julian and Blair when she mentioned it makes me wonder if something happened while she was in school and if the three of them were at the institute at the same time."

"I'll get Peabody on it. She's great with research. Not as dialed in as Dax but still top notch."

My heart squeezed at the mention of Dax Peters. He had become very close with us, especially when he discovered I was a witch.

"Dax is only one town away. As the police chief in Robins Pointe, I'll bet my soon-to-be award-winning cupcakes that he'd jump at the chance to get in on this interesting case."

He gave me a wink. "All cases with you are interesting." He pointed over my shoulder. "Dora is waving in your direction, and by that scowl on her face, I'd say she's fretting about something."

I glanced back, and sure enough, Dora was gesturing to my cupcakes. "She's annoyed I haven't finished frosting them, but everyone else is done."

Julian cleared his throat. "Ten minutes, contestants."

I gave Gage a quick kiss and jogged back to my station. The cupcakes weren't going to look pretty, but I was confident they'd taste great—well if the batter and frosting tasting I had done were any indication.

I used a spoon to swirl the orange buttercream on the

chocolate cranberry cupcake. It was a tad unconventional, but orange went with both cake flavors, and buttercream would be perfect even on dried toast. As the timer dinged, I tossed the spoon into the bowl and held my hands up in victory. I was done.

Daisy leaned over. "Those look amazing, but check out the smirk on Dora's face. She thinks her cupcakes have already won."

I glanced down the line to where Dora had plated her cranberry iced cakes. Too bad she had forgotten one important bit of information. The slivered almonds on the top were going to be an immediate disqualifier.

Blair pushed back her chair. It thudded as it connected with the floor. "Are you trying to kill me?"

When Dora realized what she had done, the color drained from her face. She burst into tears and rushed from the kitchen.

Daisy grinned, and under her breath, she murmured, "One down, a few more to go."

The door to the town hall banged as Dora raced through it. What the heck? I couldn't believe what I had overheard Daisy say. More to the point, what had Dora been thinking using almonds in her cupcake recipe?

Julian was clapping his hands in some feeble attempt to have the bakers focus on him. Frankie gave Daisy a saucy wink. Had they somehow conspired to get Dora out the door, literally?

Geoff stared at the cupcakes Dora had plated. He picked one up and bit it in half. White frosting stuck to the end of his nose. He smacked his lips together. "Too bad she used almonds and almond flour. This could have won her the round."

My ears perked up. "Almond flour, too?"

He pointed to the glass container. It was labeled *A Flour,* but the A was almost illegible.

Daisy said, "She must not have remembered that Blair is allergic to nuts and Julian to the almond flour."

I slipped my hands into the pockets of my apron. I itched to cast a spell to freeze the scene. It was a spell I had recently learned. If I could turn back time, maybe I'd understand why Dora had made the mistake of using the wrong ingredients. I cleared my throat. "This doesn't make any sense. Especially given that we all saw what happens when someone who has a severe allergy ingests the substance. It can be deadly."

I took my plate of cupcakes and placed them before the judges. Without making a statement to anyone, I hurried after Dora. If no one else was concerned about why she used almonds, I intended to find out.

Pausing on the bottom step, the icy wind whizzed down the back of my sweater, and a shiver raced down my spine. I wished I'd grabbed my jacket. I needed to stop racing out the door at the drop of a hat. Dora was huddled on a bench across the street in the town square, not wearing a jacket either. Since I was now outside, I figured it was safe. Whispering into the wind, I placed my hands behind my back. "In the cold wind of the north, I must bring forth a plea. Warm jackets for Dora and me. For this I wish so shall it be."

I felt the weight of the coats in my hands and quickly slipped my arms through my jacket sleeves and jogged across the street to Dora.

Heartbreaking sobs drifted to me as I grew closer. "Dora." I held out her jacket. "I thought you might need this."

She looked up. Her eyes were rimmed crimson, and her cheeks were wet.

I pulled a tissue from my pocket. "Here. Dry your eyes." I sat down next to her with my hands clasped in my lap and waited until the hiccups lessened. "Do you want to talk about what happened?"

With a shrug, she said, "Honestly, I don't know. One minute, I'm putting sugar crystals on the cranberries for the tops of the cupcakes, wiping down my station. The next moment, I see slivered almonds tucked around the berries. How could I be totally oblivious to hurting someone in the process of trying to win? What kind of person does that make me."

She didn't pose the last statement as a question; it was more resigned. "Do you think you were just caught up in the moment and got carried away with the final touches on your cupcakes?"

Fresh tears appeared on her lashes. "Frankie and I had been talking about how it was a shame the judges had allergies. This is the first time I've had to deal with it. I understand Blair's allergy must have recently come to light since she's been a judge at other events. It's never been an issue before." She grasped my hand and squeezed hard. "Lily, you have to believe me. I would never have knowingly hurt her, or Julian for that matter. I was in the contest to win the prize money and get that stupid blue ribbon, not to cause harm."

A few months ago, I discovered magicians used the power of suggestion on people. Could one of the other contestants have influenced Dora to use the ingredients? Or was there a witch pulling out all the stops to win, even if that meant getting excellent bakers disqualified by unorthodox means and hurting people in the process?

"Dora, you need to come back inside and apologize to the judges for what happened. You don't need to explain why, but they need to hear that from you so you won't be barred from future events. You could tell them you just pulled the wrong flour jar from the shelf and garnishes selection."

Her brow furrowed as her eyes narrowed. "What do you mean the wrong flour? I selected all-purpose flour for the cupcakes. I like to create my recipes, so I don't need as many different types of flour on my pantry shelves. The only difference is the crumb of the cake."

"Geoff showed me the container of flour you used. It was A Flour. Isn't that almond?"

Her shoulders drooped. "No. Just all-purpose. The almond flour has an illustration of a nut on the label. If Geoff is implying that I did, it's not a stretch to say he was the one easing me out the door."

I thought back to Daisy, Frankie, and Geoff. They were pleased with this turn of events. Which contestant could have dropped the almond slivers on the cupcakes while tidying his or her workstation?

Chapter 11
Lily

After a fifteen-minute delay while Dora spoke privately with the judges, it was time to hear how the remaining contestants fared.

Fred Wickshire stood. It was a nice change from Julian lording over the event. That man rubbed me the wrong way.

"May I have your attention, please?" Fred waited for all eyes to be riveted on him. "Due to the event earlier today, my fellow judges and I have decided to award points to each of the four cupcake entries. There is a thirty-point total. The balance of the seventy points will be on the final baked item, which Chef Blair will announce shortly. Each cupcake will be evaluated in three categories. Presentation, crumb, and taste. As you know, we're hoping for some creativity and complexity of flavors. If each contestant will plate your cupcake and deliver them to us, we'll begin evaluating them." He held out my plate, which I had left on the judge's table, before following Dora outside. "Lily?"

After hearing that someone may have tampered with Dora's, I was glad I moved them. I took the plate from Fred and went back to my station. I placed three chocolate cranberry cupcakes with orange buttercream on the plates, and I waited until I was invited to deliver them.

Blair said, "You may have a seat with your friends and family while we confer." I was thrilled to sit down. I had much to tell Gage and Nikki. Geoff, Frankie, and Daisy left the baking center together and headed in the direction of the coffee table.

I went in the opposite direction and bobbed my head for Gage and Nikki to follow me. Sharon Peabody and Mac Sullivan were on the other side of the room. What I needed to say wasn't for their ears.

Gage said, "Things seem to be tense up there. What's going on?"

I placed my hand on his arm. "Hold that thought." Facing Nikki, I asked, "Is there a chance you were watching Dora right before the almond incident?"

"No. I was focused on what you were doing, which, by the way, those cupcakes look amazing. I'm hoping there's one left over so I can try it."

"Thanks. Baking without magic isn't as intimidating as I made it out in my mind." I shrugged. "I need to figure out what was where when Dora was cleaning up her station. She is adamant she didn't put the almonds on her cupcakes. After she decorated them with the sugared cranberries, she cleaned up, and a few moments later, there were almonds on them. Geoff tried to tell me Dora used almond flour, too. Which, of course, I'm sure the judges heard. That would have put Julian and Blair on edge. I just don't get it. They all have the same chance of winning, and right now, with a five-way race, it's anyone's guess. Well, except now there are points involved, so it's really who gains the most points." I knew I was rambling, but this normally happened when I had too much in my brain and don't have my clue board where I can make notes and organize my thoughts. "Another interesting tidbit— Dora said that Blair has never had allergies. That's another angle that needs to be checked out. Aren't allergies diagnosed as children?"

I sagged against the wall as exhaustion crashed over me like waves during a Nor'easter, and it wasn't even noon yet.

Gage said, "I'll check into the allergy question with Blair. But all of what you've uncovered so far doesn't lead us any closer to who tried to kill Roy."

Nikki said, "If any magic had been used today, I would have picked up on the energy. Before everyone got here, I cast a spell to detect if any had been used. I wanted to make sure you had a fair chance at winning this event."

I placed a hand over my heart and it pinged. "You really believe I can win this event?"

"You have just as much chance to win this as anyone else. They're all good bakers, but so are you. I've been paying attention. You've learned the techniques you needed. You measure every ingredient with precision, which is key to baking. Other than the oven shutting down yesterday, you've been rocking it."

"It's because I had great teachers."

She laughed softly. "I'll take the compliment on behalf of your tutors." Her gaze drifted to the three others who were now sipping hot beverages. "Something is off about that trio. I can't put my finger on it. Be careful when you make your pie. I wish you could put up a protection spell around yourself as you bake, but in lieu of that, I'm going to watch everything with an eagle eye. No one will be able to mess with your final entry."

Julian rang his bell and called the bakers back to our spots.

"Gage, you'll check into Blair? Also, can you see if Roy's better? I want to be able to talk with him."

"I'll call. I agree he's an important part of this. The key to what happened is sitting in this room."

I looked to where he pointed: the contestants and judges. Well, not Fred. He had come into this after Roy had taken sick. "I've got to get up there. I'll let you know if I hear anyone spilling the beans."

Nikki gave me a hug and whispered in my ear. "Sugar cookie crust."

I had to chuckle. It was going to be my secret weapon in this battle of bakers.

Gage hugged me tight. "I'll see what I can find out. By the time you're done here, we'll have clues to review at your place before the dinner party."

I didn't have time to chat with my family and Gage's parents. Instead, I waved in their direction as I made my way back to my station. But first, the results of the cupcakes.

Once again, Fred took the lead. "Bakers, I'm happy and surprised to announce that this is a close Bake-Off. Geoff, you have twenty-four points, Daisy, twenty-six, Frankie, twenty-four, and Lily, a solid twenty-five points."

Julian said, "Congratulations to all. Now, for the final item in this first annual Pembroke Cove Bake-Off, please bake a pie. It must serve eight people, and the main ingredient is cranberries. Bakers, you will have two hours and fifteen minutes to prep, bake, cool, and serve. This time, the dessert must be plated as if we have just enjoyed a feast in a fancy restaurant, so presentation matters. Your time begins ... now."

.   .   .

I creamed butter and sugar and mixed in the flour and eggs to get the cookie dough done first since it needed to chill before I could form the crust. Once it was secured in plastic wrap and in the refrigerator, I moved on to slicing apples and creating the filling with maple syrup and a couple of secret spices that Nancy had shared with me. I was excited to see how it would compare to the other bakers. I stole a look at the workstations and saw they were rolling out pie crusts. I didn't doubt myself. This pie was a game changer in this competition, or I had to believe it was.

I slid my pie into the oven and set the timer. All I had left to do was wait for the time to be up. My fellow contestants had cleaned up their work areas and seemed to migrate to each other. I did the same, always curious as to what they might share that could be useful as we solved the current mystery.

Frankie said, "I'm glad Dora is out of the Bake-Off. She's a formidable opponent, and it will be much easier to come out on top with her gone."

Daisy and Geoff looked at each other. "What makes you think you're going to win? There are two others equally as qualified." She cast a glance in my direction, "And Lily's still in the race."

"Thanks for including me, Daisy." Even though it felt more like a slight than an inclusion, I wasn't about to let on what I really thought. I pulled up a stool and sat in the circle with them. We were away from the bright lights of the stage, and sitting together like this; the veterans of baking contests were gossiping, or as Aunt Mimi would say, *spilling the tea.*

She gave me a smile. "Of course. You're one of us now."

Frankie crossed his legs, his hands folded in his lap. It was baffling how he looked so relaxed on such an uncomfortable seat. "Lily, do you think you'll enter more competitions since you've made it this far in the Cranberry Bakery?"

As much as I wanted to seem nonchalant about the event, I could feel the color rise in my cheeks. "I don't think so. This has been fun, but I've found it to be stressful."

"For a novice, you've done pretty well," Geoff said.

"I appreciate that. My skills are limited, and what I've accomplished took tremendous planning." I left out lots of practice. Since the conversation seemed to be congenial, I asked, "Do you think Roy, Julian, and Blair will work together again?"

Daisy said, "Are you kidding? I think the three of them thrive on antagonizing each other. It's that love-hate relationship. Don't let Blair fool you; she loves to poke the bear, a.k.a. Julian, who in turn uses Roy as the buffer."

"What about the dead rat thing in her Portland location? Blair's convinced it was Julian."

Frankie shook his head. "Julian might be a lot of things, but he'd never deliberately destroy Blair. Roy either."

I looked around to make sure we were truly alone. "Do you think either Julian or Blair would have doctored Roy's coffee which caused him to go into anaphylactic shock?"

Geoff leaped up from the stool, which banged against the wall with a thud. "I'm not going to sit here and listen to you question the morals of these good people. They've given a lot back to the amateur baking world. What happened to Roy was an accident."

Daisy's head was bobbing so fast I thought it might pop off. "Did you know that Blair donates all the items left at the end of the day from her bakeries to local food pantries and shelters? That doesn't sound like a woman who would harm a friend."

I had to poke them a bit more. "What about Julian? Do you think he's capable of harming someone?"

Geoff glared at me. "All of a sudden, you're trying to pin this on one of the judges. Are you afraid you're about to lose the competition, and throwing shade at them is a way to feel better about yourself?"

I hadn't been prepared for the staunch support of the original judges. This was fascinating.

Before I could respond, Geoff said, "We've been involved with these contests for years, and Blair, Julian, and Roy have participated many times. They might snipe at each other from time to time, but they're good people. Even if one of them made a tiny mistake like handing Roy the wrong coffee, it couldn't have been intentional."

The change in the tone of Geoff's voice was unmistakable. As he talked, I knew doubt had begun to creep in. He had used the word couldn't instead of wouldn't.

"I need to check on my pie." He whirled around. Before moving back to his station, he gave his friends a pointed look. "You should check on your entry, too. These ovens can be tricky, and you don't want an overly browned crust."

A ding from my old-fashioned timer was music to my ears. I dragged the stool back to my area and grabbed the oven mitts. I eased open the door. The aroma of the sweet cookie crust wafted out and teased my taste buds. If this tasted half as good as it smelled, it would be on our Thanksgiving table this year. Who knows, it might even become a tradition.

I pulled the rack out and tested the apple using the tip of a paring knife. It slid in as if it were a hot knife going into cold butter. I eased it out further and exhaled a sigh of relief. My crust was golden with a sprinkling of coarse sugar, causing it to have a slight sparkle. This was going to look beautiful on the holly berry plates I borrowed from my aunt Mimi.

But first, I needed to cool the pie so the filling wouldn't run out from the crust. I set the pan on the granite counter. It was cool enough to speed along the process. While waiting to cut the pie, I brewed some tea that was my mother's fall harvest blend in a matching teapot. Placing the pot and cups on a tray in addition to the plates and forks with the finishing touch, cranberry-colored damask napkins, I was ready. What I might lack in baking experience I could make up for with the presentation.

I could see Mom and Aunt Mimi nodding their approval. I gave them a confident smile. No matter what happened next, over the last two days, I had accomplished baking a pie, cupcakes, muffins, and biscotti and stayed in this competition as a contender. I drew my shoulders back and stood tall. This was a moment I'd never forget.

Julian clanged his bell. "Contestants prepare to deliver your pies to the judges' table. Lily, we'll take your pie first."

I walked around the end of the counter and carefully made my way across the stage, balancing the tray that held my dessert. I placed the teacups and dessert plates in front of each judge.

"The pie is a cranberry apple compote with a sugar cookie crust. To compliment your dessert, I'm serving a harvest blend tea from MRM Teas. I hope you enjoy it."

I turned away and held up my fist in victory, away from the judges' eyes but enough for my family and friends to see. Gage whistled, and everyone in the audience gave me an enthusiastic round of applause.

When I returned to my spot, I watched as each judge took a bite of my pie. I held my breath. My heart rate ticked up, and I wiped the palms of my hands on my apron.

Julian looked at Blair, who in turn scowled at me. Fred was the only judge who seemed to be enjoying my pie.

Julian stood up, his hands clenched at his sides. "Lily. How dare you use one of my recipes in this contest." He glared at me. "My filling and the cookie crust is Blair's creation. Did you think cheating was the way to win?"

I felt the color drain from my face. Stammering, I said, "Chef Julian. I didn't. I wouldn't. I promise."

Shaking her fist, Nancy stormed across the room. Through gritted teeth she said, "It was never either of your recipes. They were mine."

Chapter 12
Gage

The minute Nancy shouted the recipes were hers and not Julian's or Blair's, I jumped to my feet. Lily had said Nancy confided in her that she had been in culinary school. I was still waiting on confirmation from Peabody as to when, and if the three of them had been in school together.

Threading my way around people, I shot her off a text. *Information is needed now on Nancy Litchfield.*

Bubbles like she was typing appeared on my screen. They stopped and then came back. *NL was at CIA with J and B.* That was the culinary school she had alluded to when she talked with Lily. I hopped up on the small platform.

In those few short minutes between her announcement and right now, Julian's face drained of color, and Blair was slumped in her chair. This wasn't the reaction I would have expected. Julian had shown he was a presence to be reckoned with, and Blair appeared to be a tough business-woman. Both were half the person they had been moments before.

Lily rushed over and pushed her hands in the pockets of her apron. I could see her fists were balled. "I can assure you the recipe I made was not taken from either of you. When I decided to enter this contest, a few of my friends came together to help me since I was a novice baker. I reviewed the rules, and nowhere did it state the recipes had to be original. I just had to bake them." She gestured to the pie slices on the table. "I didn't cheat."

Julian's eyes bored into Nancy. "Lily, you may not have done anything wrong, but she's trying to besmirch our reputations." He jabbed his finger in Nancy's direction. "There's a reason you washed out of the CIA."

"We know it wasn't my fault. One of you set me up to take the fall for your mistake. I was caught in the crossfire. All these years I watched as the two of you rose in fame and fortune. I was living in my hometown with nothing but a tattered reputation so that no culinary school would touch me."

Blair smacked her hand on the table. It drew everyone's attention to her. "That's a far cry from what really happened. Do you want me to share the truth in front of everyone in this room?"

Nancy shrunk in retreat at Blair's venom-laced words.

I held up my hands, one in each of the women's directions. "This is a conversation best kept until the conclusion of today's events." Giving each woman and Julian a pointed look. "I'll be the mediator, and we'll discuss it at the station." This would give me an opportunity to see if this long-simmering feud was related to what happened to Roy Fletcher. Some might say it was coincidental, but I didn't think coincidence was a viable explanation when a crime had been committed. "For now, let's conclude the contest, award the winner, and allow these good people who are in attendance to enjoy what's left of their weekend."

Julian hadn't backed down from his aggressive stance. "How can we fairly judge this contest knowing it's been tainted?"

Lily looked between the judges and Nancy. "I've acted in good faith. Why wouldn't you judge my pie based on the flavors and execution of the presentation? That's what you should do if you want to be fair."

Daisy, Geoff, and Frankie had remained silent as Lily spoke up in her defense. I wasn't sure which way they'd go. If she were eliminated, it would help them get one step closer to declaring victory.

"You should ask the other contestants what they would do if they were in your shoes."

Frankie huddled the other two close to him. I could see his mouth moving but couldn't hear what he said. Lily's fate of staying in the contest rested in their hands since the judges weren't about to support her.

Frankie nodded and turned to address the judges. "We've talked it over, and if you disqualify Lily because of a personal issue from college between the three of you, then you'll do a disservice to her and us. We believe she should remain in the competition, even though it means we have a one-in-four chance of winning."

Lily stood a little straighter. Her face melted into a grateful smile. She mouthed thank you to them before Julian announced his decision.

Blair tipped her head in Lily's direction as if she agreed with Frankie.

Fred said, "Lily's pie is not the issue. She didn't try to pass off the recipe as her original creation." He paused. If there had been a cartoon bubble above his head, it might have read, *like you've been accused of doing*. "She must remain in this contest."

Julian threw up his hands. "Fine. She can stay." He jabbed his index finger in Nancy's direction. "Stick around. Our conversation isn't over yet."

Nancy thrust her chin up. "I'm not going anywhere. It's time this was resolved once and for all."

My cell phone buzzed with an incoming message. I turned away from the group and scanned it. I clenched my jaw and acknowledged the text. *Thank you for the update.* Lily was watching me as I stowed the phone. I slowly shook my head and never broke eye contact with her. There would be time soon enough to tell her that Roy Fletcher died from a massive heart attack.

I tapped the tabletop and gave Fred, Julian, and Blair my best cop stare. "Judges, proceed with the contest. We'll sort everything out at the conclusion of the event." Two of the three judges, including Nancy, would be accompanying me to the station for questioning. I knew in my gut this contest was linked to Roy's death. It was up to me and my detectives to figure out how.

Stepping out of the center of the dais, I strode to the back of the room, where Peabody and Mac were lingering. She inclined her head to the door. I nodded. Mac held the door as we walked through it. I needed to make this quick since I wanted to see if Lily won.

"What's going on, Detective?" Mac asked.

"I got a text from Dr. Hammond. Roy Fletcher died about an hour ago. The doctor said the heart attack was the result of stress placed on his body due to anaphylaxis. Then, the attempted smothering didn't help. During the night, monitoring indicated that Roy's heart showed distress. When he went into cardiac arrest, they did all they could, but he succumbed. As soon as Lily's done with this contest, you know she'll be in the thick of this investigation. But we need to rely on what she might have seen or heard over the last two days."

Peabody said, "Agreed. In addition, she's a valuable asset in these types of cases."

It was an interesting way to avoid stating the obvious that we'd had more than our share of homicides in Pembroke Cove. "I'm going to head back in, keep a sharp eye on things. Once this event is over, escort Nancy, Julian, Fred, and Blair to the station. This hostility between everyone but Fred is curious, and with a bit of luck, he might have heard something."

"You got it, boss." Mac pulled open the door so that we could reenter the event.

From the look at the dessert plates in front of the judges and half-eaten pie slices, I guessed the winner would be declared any time now. I had my fingers crossed for Lily, but she had said she didn't care if she won. I was proud of her no matter what. Trying something new was always a plus for anyone.

The judges spoke in hushed tones. Julian's face was flushed as he shook his head and tapped the clipboard he was holding. Blair's lips thinned, seemingly at odds with Julian, which didn't surprise me after seeing them interact over the last two days.

He placed his clipboard to the side of the plate and rose to his feet. He took a step back, and his trademark grin appeared. It was interesting how easily he could flip moods.

"May I have your attention, please? After much debate and quite a lively and unforgettable contest, we've selected a winner. However, before I announce third place to first, I'd like to say that each baker who competed is a winner.

Baking is an art form. The baker must also be part chemist, as a balance of ingredients is critical for the final outcome. Therefore, I award third place to Daisy Patton for her Cranberry Pumpkin Pie with a gingersnap crust."

Applause filled the room as Daisy crossed from the baking center to accept her white ribbon and shake the judges' hands.

From where I was standing, I saw she blinked away tears. I guessed from disappointment and not happiness.

Julian once again cleared his throat to draw the attention back to himself. "Second place," he leaned toward the remaining contestants and said, "Can you feel the excitement yet?"

Someone in the back grumbled, "Get on with it."

Julian glanced at the crowd, frowned, and said, "Second place goes to Geoff Marks for his Cranberry Chiffon Pie."

Lily and Frankie stepped closer together as Geoff accepted his ribbon and took his place next to Daisy.

Julian joked. "We're down to two, but can you guess who's the winner?"

He held up Lily's plate with her cranberry apple pie, which I thought looked amazing. The ruby red of the cranberries nestled in between thinly sliced apple and the sugar cookie crust. I knew it was a flavor sensation; even if she didn't get first place, it was the best. Then he held aloft Frankie's plate. From where I stood, it didn't look like a pie; more like a cake.

"Both of these were excellent. However, Frankie may call his dessert cranberry pie, but it's reminiscent of a cake. Therefore, our winner is Lily Michaels with her Cranberry Apple Pie with a Sugar Cookie Crust."

Frankie gave Lily a hug and stepped back. Her hand flew to cover her open mouth as her cheeks flamed deep pink. I longed to run up and throw my arms around her in congratulations, but this was her moment to savor. Julian waved her over to the table.

She moved at a turtle pace for the first two steps and then hurried over. "Chef Julian, are you sure?"

"As much as I hate to admit this, Nancy was right to goad us into letting you continue in the competition. You've baked an excellent pie."

Lily accepted the blue ribbon and an envelope.

Caiden Piper jumped to his feet. "Lily, can I take your picture for the Pembroke Edge?"

She smoothed down the front of her apron. "Yes."

He took several pictures of her alone, holding a plate with the winning pie, with the judges, and finally with the three other contestants. "I appreciate your patience, everyone. Look for my article in the next edition of the newspaper."

I hopped up to the platform and slipped my arm around her waist, kissing her cheek. "Congratulations, Sweetheart. It looks like you now have a signature pie."

She laughed and kissed me.

Blair came over and shook her hand. "Excellent job, Lily, on all your creations, not just the pie. It's interesting how you combined the filling from Julian and me with an added twist to the sugar cookie base that I can't quite place. It's a borderline Snickerdoodle crust and like nothing I've ever tasted before. If you wouldn't mind sharing your recipe, I'd love to feature it in my bakeries for our Christmas pie selection."

"Really. My pie?" Lily's sable brown eyes grew big as saucers. "Yeah, sure, I'd be happy to."

Blair inclined her head. "Of course, there is a small compensation, and you'll need to give me the right to distribute it exclusively. You wouldn't be able to allow anyone else," she glanced over her shoulder to where Julian was talking with Fred, "to include it in a cookbook, for example."

Before Lily could respond, Mimi strolled up. "Well done, my dear." She gave Blair a pointed look. "Before Lily decides about her pie recipe, she needs time to consider your offer."

Blair narrowed her eyes and gave Mimi a harsh look. "You realize this is a way for Lily to make a little money. In addition, it will save me time from deconstructing the pie and creating a new recipe."

"If you thought you could discover what she used you wouldn't have asked. Her pie is unique, and before she hands out any recipe, she'll think about it." Mimi punctuated her statement with a firmness that usually didn't slip out in casual conversation.

"Whatever." Blair handed her business card to Lily. "I'm leaving."

I gestured for Peabody and Mac to come forward. "There are several matters we need to discuss which includes a trip to the police station."

Once Lily had been declared the winner, most of the room emptied quickly. A few of our friends and family were waiting to congratulate Lily, but I needed to corral my suspects. "May I have all the contestants from yesterday and today come to the judges' area?" If anyone had left, I could bring them in for questioning later. This would be the most expeditious way to share the news about Roy Fletcher and get their collective reactions.

I waited until all the critical people were in front of me. It was odd that it looked like a lineup of suspects. Lily stood next to me. Her fingertips grazed my hand. I gave hers a quick squeeze. She stood straighter and was prepared for what was to come.

"I received a message about Roy Fletcher." I scanned the group, and no one moved a muscle. "He died earlier this morning. His death is now officially a homicide."

Daisy cried, "NO," and collapsed to the floor.

Chapter 13
Lily

I rushed forward and helped Daisy to a nearby chair. Nikki gave her a glass of water. Over the next thirty minutes, it was controlled chaos. The contestants and judges, standing in front of Gage when he announced Roy Fletcher's death, were on their way to the police station. Most were walking the short distance from the town hall to the station since they bookended the town square.

I kept my arm around Daisy's shoulders as she continued to sip water. I was concerned as her hands were clammy and she was as pale as a ghost.

"Daisy, are you sure you want to walk? Nikki has her car out front."

She straightened up, shrugged my arm away, and pulled the elastic from her ponytail to massage the back of her head. "The fresh air will help. I'm sorry I fainted, but hearing about Roy," a shudder raced over her body, "was a shock." She glanced around the mostly empty room. "I-I had feelings for him, and now he'll never know." Daisy buried her face in her hands as her blonde hair fell around her cheeks like a closed curtain while she cried softly.

I looked at Nikki. That was a surprise. Discovering Daisy cared for Roy on top of learning about his death was almost enough to leave me speechless, but not quite. "He didn't know how you felt about him?"

She peeked between her fingers. "I just couldn't tell him. He was so kind, smart, and handsome. Way out of my league."

Nikki handed her a tissue. Her voice was devoid of emotion. "Dry your eyes. The detectives will wonder where we are if we don't get to the station soon."

We were going to be the good cop, bad cop version in addition to crackerjack sleuths. Helping Daisy to her feet, I winked at Nikki. "Daisy, where's your coat?"

"In the back storage room." She gestured to where the cups had been found yesterday.

"What color is it, and I will get it for you?" This would also give me an opportunity to take another look before we left.

"It's bright yellow, like a rain slicker, only a winter coat."

"You should collect any tools you brought with you. I'll meet you in the baking center in just a couple of minutes."

Nikki said, "I'll pick up your area, Lily."

The two of us went in different directions while Daisy continued to sit in the chair. I glanced over my shoulder as I entered the storage room and tugged on the rope for the solitary overhead light. The room was flooded in a harsh white light. I wasn't sure if there was anything left to see, but it never hurt to look around.

One shelf was loaded with normal cleaning supplies, including rolls of paper towels and more sleeves of plain white coffee cups. The next shelf to the right held town pamphlets, maps, and boxes of pens printed with Pembroke

Cove on them. The coat rack was to the left of the door, and Daisy's coat was the only one hanging on the peg. I withdrew my phone and took a series of pictures of the room and each shelf and cubby area to examine more closely later.

I picked up her coat, and on the peg, a piece of paper was pushed over it. A note. I took several pictures from both sides and a close-up in case it tore. Then, holding it by the corner, I carefully removed the tattered page. Scrawled in bold letters with dark green marker, it said, *I KNOW WHAT YOU DID.*

Turning it over, the back side was blank. Was this message for Daisy or someone else? Taking a quick picture, I sent it off to Gage with a text. *I found this under Daisy's coat. Should I bag it and bring it in?*

YES!! I chuckled at his response. I magicked up a Ziploc bag and slipped it inside. I was happy that my spell worked flawlessly, but I had more than my fair share of practice needing baggies.

I stuck the bag under my sweater since I didn't want Daisy to see it and have to explain. Gage could question her about it. The element of surprise was an excellent tool when he was talking with a potential suspect. Thinking about my last thought, could she be a potential suspect in Roy's death? Even if she said she cared for him, I had seen that story play out once before with a relationship that had been faked all to coerce someone into doing what they wanted. In the end, the final outcome had been murder. I didn't want to contemplate that this could be a similar scenario.

Nancy waved to us as she got into her car. I returned the gesture and was impressed she had given her statement so quickly. She must have been the first to talk with the officers. Daisy's steps slowed as we mounted the cement steps to the police station. When we reached the top, she extended a shaking hand to the door handle and froze. "I can't go in there."

It was up to me to get her in the door and ready to talk with Gage and the other detectives. "Daisy, I know this is scary. To talk with the police about what you might have seen over the last two days, but do it because it's the right thing to do. Help the police find the person responsible for Roy's death."

Her watery blue eyes were wide. "I want to help if I can, but I don't know anything. I was there to bake, not observe what others were doing."

"Our brains are like mini film recorders. It remembers everything, even if we're unaware. Besides Gage is very easy to talk with."

She grabbed my hand and sunk her fingertips into the fleshy part of my palm. "Stay with me. You know I wouldn't have hurt Roy. I could use a friendly face in the room."

"We'll need to check with Gage. I won't be able to speak while I'm in the room with you, but I'd be happy to give you moral support if he agrees."

She threw her arms around me and hugged me tight. "Thank you, Lily. You're such a nice person. I hope we can be friends when this is all over. Even though I live in Drake's Bay, it's just an hour south of Pembroke Cove."

"That would be nice."

Nikki cleared her throat. "We should get inside."

Daisy grasped the door handle and tugged. Fred Wickshire was on the opposite side, giving it a push.

He dipped his head, "Ladies." and hurried down the steps.

It didn't surprise me that he was in and out quickly. Fred hadn't been at the event when Roy collapsed and only came to help so the contest could continue. "I'll be right back."

I ran down the steps and called to Fred. "Hold up a minute?"

His steps slowed, and he faced me. "Lily, I would have stopped to congratulate you, but I saw you were with Daisy. I didn't want to rub salt in her wound. I'm very happy you won today. What Julian and Blair wanted to do wasn't fair."

"Thank you, Fred. I appreciate your support. I wanted to ask if you could put a dozen and a half of your delicious rolls aside for me. I can pick them up later this afternoon and maybe a couple of quarts of lobster bisque." It was a little heavy to go with my current dinner menu, but I needed an excuse to chat with him later.

"Of course. I'm always happy to prepare a to-go order for you. What time do you think you'll be by the restaurant?"

"Would four thirty be okay? I have some folks coming for dinner. Your rolls and bisque would put my party over the top."

He chuckled. "Flattery will get you a little added bonus, you know."

"That's not necessary, but when it's true..." I deliberately let my sentence hang in the air. Would he pick up the thread of things based on truth?

He looked over my shoulder to Daisy, standing with Nikki, still holding the door ajar. It was obvious Daisy did not want to walk inside.

Fred said, "There's one girl who is worth taking a hard look at."

"Why do you say that?" I stuck my chilled hands in my coat pockets.

"Two nights ago, Roy Fletcher was alone at the Clam Bake, enjoying a quiet dinner. He was just cracking the first lobster claw when that one sauntered up and slid into the booth across from him. She waved to me. I went over, and she announced she would join Roy for dinner and asked if I could bring her what he was having."

I smiled at how he said lobsta instead of lobster. A true native. "Did you get the impression she arrived late?"

He frowned. "Nope. By Roy's open-mouthed look of shock, I'd say definitely not."

"And you delivered her meal?"

"I put the order in. When I went to ask her what she'd like to drink, Roy announced there had been a change of plans, and Daisy wouldn't be staying. And get this, would I pack her order to go?" His heavy Maine accent punctuated each word. "I can tell you that he was not happy with the situation, and because of the sourpuss look on her face, neither was she. Being told to leave must have been humiliating."

"I'm sure it was. Did you notice anything else while she was at his table?"

"They talked for a few minutes. Well, I should say she talked while he shook his head. I put a rush on her meal to get Roy out of the jam he seemed to be stuck in. When I brought her food over, she snatched it out of my hand, jabbed a finger in his direction and said, *you might come to regret this conversation.* She didn't wait for him to respond and stormed out."

This was very interesting. Daisy could have told Roy she had feelings for him, but he might not have reciprocated. "What did Roy say after she left?"

"Nothing, really. Just thanked me for expediting her order to get her out of there. I left the man in peace to enjoy what was left of his dinner. But I'm not sure that he did. He was all slumped over his plate and didn't look like a man enjoying a good lobster."

"Did anyone else join Roy?"

"No. I gave him a dessert on the house. Maybe an hour later, he left. But the kicker, her dinner was on the hood of his car when he went out."

"How do you know that?"

"He brought it in. Handed it to me in case she came back and claimed it. I knew it was hers since I had written the table number on the bag."

"Interesting." The brain cells had kicked in, and I was churning over clues that needed to go on my board. "Thanks for your time Fred. I'll see you later."

"If you think of anything else you need, just call. I'll have everything ready for you by four twenty, just in case you're a tad early."

"Fred, you're a gem." I touched him on the arm.

By the time I walked up the steps, Nikki had convinced Daisy to go indoors. When I walked in, Julian and Blair were sitting on opposite sides of the room. Geoff and Dora were next to each other, and Frankie was nowhere to be seen. I assumed he was sharing his side of the story in one of the interrogation rooms.

Daisy sat in a chair away from the others. I wished I could tell Nikki what Fred had shared with me, but Gage needed to hear it first so he could prepare his questions accordingly.

Alice, a sweet-faced young lady, was at the front desk. I gave her a warm smile. It was unusual to have this many people waiting to talk with an officer, let alone about the same case.

"Hi, Alice, is Gage free?"

"Hey, Lily, I'm not sure, but I'll check. Hold on half a sec." She picked up the handset on the desk phone and tapped in three digits. Seconds later she said, "Gage, Lily's here, and she's asked to see you right quick."

He must have picked up on the first ring.

"All right, she's on her way." She hung up and bobbed her head in the direction of his office. "He said come on back."

"Thanks, Alice."

I slipped down the hallway avoiding Daisy. It was better she didn't see me instead of getting worried about what I might be doing. Especially since she didn't know what Fred had shared with me.

I sailed through the door to Gage's office and went around the desk. Giving him a quick kiss on the cheek, I said, "I'll make this short and sweet."

He leaned back in his chair, steepled his fingertips together, and grinned. "Nice to see you too. I'm guessing you have information."

I winked. "I do. I bumped into Fred outside, and before you chat with Daisy, I wanted to make sure you had all the interesting details about two nights ago. Did you know that she joined Roy for dinner at the Clam Bake, uninvited? And did you know that he wasn't happy about it? And did you know that she left her to-go bag on the hood of his car? Like, who does that with a lobster dinner? That's a downright sin to waste a good Maine lobster." I took a breath after rattling off the questions without taking one.

He patted the desktop. "Breathe, my favorite witch."

I smiled and sat on the corner and took a deep breath.

He placed his hand on my knee. "Fred gave me all the details about Roy and Daisy."

"What you don't know is that she told me and Nikki that she had feelings for Roy. Now that he was dead, she'd never have the chance to tell him." I snapped my fingers together. "What if they talked about that, and he rejected her? He was judging the competition, and she was a contestant, not just in this event but in others. Roy was a passionate foodie."

"This is an excellent hypothesis. For the record, I plan on discussing all of this with her. Peabody will be in the room."

"About that, Daisy asked if I could join her when she's being questioned. And after talking with Fred, I'd like to be in the room, but a better use of my time would be to get home and update the clue board before I forget any details. Is there a way you can phrase it so I can ease out of it?"

He blinked hard. "Let me get this straight—you don't want to be there when I question my prime suspect."

I nodded. "That's just it, Gage. She's too obvious. I think whoever doctored Roy's coffee and tried to smother him wasn't Daisy Patton. Whoever did had a motive that had nothing to do with unrequited love."

He stood and kissed me tenderly. "I've got this. You head home and work on the board, and we can discuss this tonight."

"Good, then you'll know where to find me and Nikki. In addition to setting up the clues and reviewing everything that's happened, there is a dinner party to get ready for." I cupped his cheek and said, "Don't forget dinner is at five thirty, so don't be late, any of you."

"Yes, dear."

Sharon stuck her head in the office after a quick tap on

the door. "Detective, I'm ready to question Daisy Patton. Are you coming?"

"Right behind you. Before we begin, we have to get Lily off the hook as Daisy's moral support."

She grinned. "You want to miss an interrogation?"

I couldn't help but laugh. "I know it's highly unusual, so make sure to write it down. Oh, and I just reminded Gage, but wrap up here in plenty of time to get ready for tonight. It's going to be a great time with the gang, and remember EL is coming too."

Pink flushed her cheeks. "I won't be late, promise. Thanks, Lily."

"Sharon, it's just dinner, right?"

"Dinner. With my friends and EL."

"Come hungry. I ordered dinner rolls and bisque from the Clam Bake."

Gage held up his hand. "I volunteer for pick up."

"I might have more questions for Fred, but if I don't, that would be great."

He laughed. "Leave it to you to incorporate takeout and an investigation into your dinner party plans."

I fluttered my eyelashes and pretended to be offended. "Who me? I'm just trying to be efficient. Isn't that what a good sleuth does?"

He brushed my hair back from my eyes. "Yes, that is exactly what one does, and you're one of the best."

Chapter 14
Lily

Nikki was whipping up a seafood lasagna to complement the rolls and lobster bisque I had ordered. The beef lasagna had been wrapped and put in the freezer for another night.

I stepped back and scanned the notes I had finished on my board. "Nik, what am I missing?"

Milo slunk around the corner of the hall and hopped onto the chair. "Not reading it out loud to us is your first issue. Hearing the sound of your voice reading off the clues allows me to close my eyes and put myself at the scene of the crime, or in this case, crimes. Speaking for Nikki, she's preparing dinner." Milo tipped his head in her direction. "I, for one, thank you."

Nikki laughed. "That's only because you saw me slip a piece of salmon in a water bath to poach."

'True, but I happen to be partial to any witch who can cook better than... well, I'm not going to finish that statement."

I knelt down next to his chair. "Milo." I admonished. "I buy the delicious smoked salmon you love, bring home fish from the docks on a regular basis, and even make sure you have plenty of tuna juice."

He stood on his back paws and placed his front paws on my shoulders. Leaning in, he purred against my cheek. "My dear witch, a tiny part of my role in your life is to tease you. I don't care that you can't cook like Nikki or any other witch, for that matter. We don't starve. But if you want to take some cooking classes now that you've learned to bake, neither Gage nor I would object."

I kissed the top of his little soft head. "It's good to know I have your support. Right now, we have a murder to solve."

"Hmm." Milo purred. "Can you call it murder when it sounds like his heart gave out?"

"How did you hear that, and what else do you know?" My familiar had more details about the end of Roy's life than I did.

He placed a paw over his eyes. "You always discount my network of familiars."

I folded my arms over my chest and kept my foot from tapping on the tile floor. All that would do was annoy Milo and get him to withhold information even longer. "Because you've never introduced me to any of them."

"A familiar needs a little mystery in his life, don't you think, Nikki?"

She waved an oven-mitt covered hand in the air. "Keep me out of this. I'm neutral."

"Coward," Milo said.

"No. Just smart." She leaned her backside against the sink. "Spill the beans. What *do* you know?" She emphasized the word, *do*, to get Milo to focus.

That did the trick. Milo sat up straight on the chair and said, "My dear witch, be prepared to jot down notes. There could be a gem in what I've discovered while you were imitating Julia Child."

I picked up the chalk and inched closer to the blackboard. "First, I'll read what I have."

He said, "Good idea. It will give us the update on all that you've discovered so far."

Victim Roy Fletcher, mid-40s, single, from the Portland area. Allergy – aspartame, attempted suffocation in hospital. Self-proclaimed foodie

Missing EpiPens- Blair's and Roy's

Suspects

Blair Holt – bad blood between her and J – drinks fake sugar

Chef Julian Peppen

Daisy Patton – had fight with Roy 2 days ago, confessed to having feelings for him

Geoff Marks – close proximity – motive unclear

Frankie Thorn

Dora Ingalls

Nancy Litchfield – former culinary student with J & B – claims they stole her recipes

"Well done, Lily. This is an excellent foundation from which to kick off our investigation. Now, at this point, we don't know all the motives as to why someone would want this man dead. What I learned was the heart attack was a cumulative result of the allergy reaction, leaving him close to death. After all he was in a light coma."

"He was, but when Gage talked to the doctor last night, he was optimistic Roy would recover."

"Correct. That was before someone tried to deprive him of oxygen."

"Milo, you have an interesting way of putting things." I realized I hadn't noted that Blair and Julian were at the hospital last night. I jotted that next to their names.

Nikki crossed the room, picked up Milo, and sat down with him in her lap. "What else did you learn from your unnamed sources?"

"There's a witch who works as a nurse in the intensive care unit. So, her familiar hangs out a bit."

Milo loved the drama of sharing information and tended to drag out a story. However, I had learned not to rush him, or the snark would come out, and he'd stalk off. "Is the witch a member of our coven?" I wondered if I knew who she was.

"Yes."

After he stopped talking, I looked at Nikki, who shrugged as if agreeing that this was typical of Milo.

"As I was saying, the pseudo-girlfriend dropped by last night, and some dude named Geoff."

I perked up. "Daisy and Geoff were there. Neither of them mentioned that. I wonder if they said anything to Gage?" It was something I could ask him about later. "This information doesn't prove anything about his death. We need to go back to the beginning. Who might have doctored his coffee?" I put a star next to Blair's name. "I'm going out on a limb for conversation's sake. And bear with me."

Milo leaned toward Nikki. "She's got that Sherlock look. See how her brow is like wrinkles in a bedsheet, and her eyes are all squinty and now they're closed?"

Nikki said, "I never noticed that look before."

"Figures, you're starting to get what I call your Holmes face and body as if you're ready to learn some interesting fact."

"What are you talking about?" Nikki said.

"You inch closer to Lily and seem to shut out everything around you and focus on her. It's a good thing, Nikki. You're a good partner."

"Guys, focus. We should follow the assumption that it was Blair's coffee. Nancy had offered to fix a cup for me when I signed in yesterday. If she gave him the wrong cup by mistake, why not confess? No one would have thought another thing about it. Accidents happen."

Nikki got up and stood next to the clue board. She tapped the word EpiPen. "What about the pens? If Roy's allergy was life-threatening, shouldn't he have carried one, and didn't Blair say hers was missing, too? What if it was deliberate and the missing EpiPen was something else the killer did? Also, remember that someone put nuts on Dora's submission during the cupcake contest. That could have almost killed Blair had she ingested them."

"There is no way that Blair would have eaten them. It was easy to spot the danger." Nuts. Almonds. I had a folder full of images from the baking center. I couldn't quite put my finger on it, but something niggled at the back of my brain. Photos always helped. "It's too bad I don't have a photographic memory."

I dug through the stack of printed images on the sideboard. Triumphant, I held up a photo of a clear canister marked with a line drawing of a nut. "Look at this. Almond flour. Julian pretended to have an allergic reaction, but if Dora or any of us had used it, that would have been an intentional attempt to cause harm even though for him it's about the texture." I handed the photo to Nikki and she showed it to Milo. "I've been thinking, why on earth would you be a food judge at these kinds of events if you really were allergic to the items that might be used? It makes zero sense."

"Aspartame would never be used in baking. Roy would have been safe there." Nikki said. "If Blair's allergy is real, would she pretend to taste the items, and that made Julian or someone else mad? Since now, there wouldn't be the official tiebreaker."

"If Roy was out of the picture, Blair would have to actually taste the entries. Then she could have been slipped something with ground nuts." That was an interesting theory. "Which now makes me wonder if Julian *is* our primary suspect. He and Blair are at war over the cookbook, and he allegedly put dead rats in her bakery." I pulled out a chair and sat down. Exhaustion washed over me, and my bones didn't feel like they could hold me up another second. "I wish I could read minds."

Milo mused, "Being a witch isn't enough? Non-magicals would love to have your skills."

I snorted. "Sure, like the time I was accused of murder for my book of magic or the time I doused all the lights in Pembroke Cove trying to learn a simple spell so I didn't have to get out of bed to turn off the lights. I'm a gem of a witch."

"Turn that thinking around," Milo said, his deep kitty grumble rushing out. It was an indication he was annoyed with me. "Not only can you flick a light switch, but you can also use a wand to give yourself a flashlight. You have a book of magic that teaches you spells that help people. Like casting a protection spell around Gage when he's in danger or finding me when I had been doused with poison. Not to mention that you can clean up the kitchen with a flick of your wrist. What person wouldn't love that option?"

I scooped Milo and hugged him to my chest. "Basically, you're reminding me to be grateful for the gifts that have been bestowed on me. They're a blessing, not a curse."

He patted my cheek with his paw and purred. "Exactly. One of these days, you'll turn around the negative thoughts that creep in with positives." He squirmed from my arms and dropped to the floor. He stalked to the back door and stopped before he eased through his swinging kitty door. "If I might offer some advice—start with the coffee, who was at the hospital and who withheld that information from the police. Finally, who had time to get to the hospital before the baking contest resumed this morning? That will narrow down your suspects." After he eased out the door, it swung a couple of times in his wake.

I glanced at Nikki. "Are you up for a little visit to Nancy's house? Milo's right. It starts with that coffee, and Nancy sat near the refreshment table the entire time. With any luck, she would have seen if any one of our suspects came in late."

Nikki glanced at her watch. "We need to be back by quarter past five at the latest to make sure all is ready for the dinner party. We want to make a good impression on EL for Sharon's sake."

I held up the palm of my hand and waited for the high-five to come.

Nikki grasped my hand. "If we had capes, we'd be like the dynamic duo."

"I don't think my mini coop compares to the bat mobile, but I can roll with that comparison. They always got their man or woman."

I texted Gage to let him know we were going out for a bit and would pick up the order from the Clam Bake. Also, if by the off chance we were delayed, everything was under control here.

Nikki handed me my wool coat and waited for me to put it on. "How do you plan to approach Nancy?"

"I'm not accusing her of anything. I'll start with the coffee. I know anyone could get a cup, but it was part of her role at the event to fix coffee for the judges. After all, Chef Julian's ego is as big as the entire state of Maine. He strikes me as the type to like being waited on."

Worry lines etched into Nikki's face. "Do you think Nancy's innocent? She's been such a good friend and supporter of my baking business. I would hate to have misjudged her."

"Julian is my primary suspect. He has a motive to get rid of Blair since the feud continued about recipes, and he'd probably think Roy was a necessary casualty caught in the crossfire of a long-standing war."

I pulled open the door. "We need to talk to Nancy. And I can't wait to see what information Gage gathered today. Between the police questioning and our sleuthing, we should be able to narrow down the suspect list after dinner." I cringed as the words came out of my mouth. Usually, when I thought the case was about to break open, it went in the opposite direction.

We pulled up to Nancy's cedar shake bungalow on the south side of town. The ambulance and police cruiser pulled away from the curb. At least the lights weren't flashing. Nikki and I looked at each other. Her face was as pale as mine must have been.

"Do you think..." she began.

And I finished, "Nancy's okay?"

We pushed open our doors the moment the car was off and raced up the front walk, taking the porch steps two at a time. I banged on the door, calling her name. It might have been a tad more dramatic than necessary, but I didn't care.

The panic that had wrapped itself around my chest drove me to be a bit over the top.

When she didn't answer, I thumped harder, this time with my fist. "Nancy."

Nikki held her finger to her lips. "Wait. I think I hear her coming." She pressed her ear to the door and nodded. "Definitely footsteps." She straightened up and gave me a weak smile.

The door eased open. Nancy was still wearing the lavender sweater she wore earlier. Now the left shoulder was bright red. I assumed it was blood since she sported a large white bandage over her left eye. She leaned heavily against the door frame. She blinked a few times and looked more like an owl than I thought possible, "This is a surprise."

Chapter 15
Gage

I perched on the corner of my desk and considered the best approach with the group of people waiting in the lobby. Julian was a pompous jerk, Blair didn't seem to care much about anyone or anything other than her business, Geoff and Frankie were spouting off about the inconvenience of having to answer questions, and Dora and Daisy were the only two who sat patiently waiting their turn.

Peabody entered my office and closed the door. "We should question Daisy again now that she's had time to process the news about Mr. Fletcher's death."

"I was considering that among other lines of questioning."

She gave a nod, her lips pursed deep in thought. "Is it possible a couple of them are in this mess together? Either a contestant and judge, two contestants or the two judges?"

"It's all about the timeline and where they were last night at the time the attempted murder was happening. If I was a betting man, I'd say they'll offer up alibis for each other."

"It's a fact Julian and Blair were together at the hospital. How much time elapsed between when they were told they couldn't visit him to when the nurse discovered someone trying to smother him?"

I pulled up my phone and scanned my notes. "They arrived before visiting hours ended, so right before eight o'clock. The attempt on Roy's life was around ten. This sounds crude, but the perp should have waited until shift change when the staff gave and took report. There's less chance of a nurse or aide walking in on him or her."

"Factual, but harsh."

"Peabody, being a detective, is puzzling out different scenarios. Since we know whoever it was either didn't think about the hand-off or wasn't able to delay an hour, the next logical question would be, why? Was their alibi not an option later, that kind of thing."

"What if," she shook her head, "never mind."

"If you have an idea, spit it out. You never know how an investigation can turn with a what-if statement."

"All right, let's say whoever went to the hospital wasn't thinking clearly. They saw Mr. Fletcher lying on the bed comatose. They were the one responsible for his condition. This person panicked, having heard all the stories about people who can live in that state for years and never get better. If a nurse or doctor hadn't clued them in that Mr. Fletcher was expected to recover, on impulse, they grabbed the pillow."

"A mercy killing?" I stood up from the desk. "It's a working theory, but I don't buy it. If we knew how he got the coffee laced with aspartame, it would help." I jabbed my index finger in the direction of the lobby. "One or two of those people know what happened. It's our job to break them down and discover the truth."

"Who do you want to talk with first, Detective?"

"Dora Ingalls. I'll meet you in conference room A. I want to check in with Lily first."

Peabody gave me a smile. "I'll bet she's got her clue board out and is working on this as well."

"You've got that right. We need to make sure everyone stays in town. Call the Coastal Motel and have whoever isn't local stay there. At least this way, we'll know how to find them tomorrow."

"Consider it done." She stalked from the room.

I admired Peabody. She had a razor-sharp mind and was going to develop into an excellent detective. I hit the speed dial button for Lily, but it went straight to voicemail. I hung up and dialed again. For the second time, it went to voicemail. She was with Nikki, so I really didn't have cause to worry, but I wished she had answered. Instead, I left her a message.

"Hello, Sweetheart; I wanted to talk to you for a minute. Not to worry; the team and I will be on time for dinner. Text me if I should pick up the Clam Bake order."

I stashed my phone as I entered the conference room. Dora was sitting at the wooden table, her hands folded in her lap until she tugged on the hem of her sweatshirt. She then ruffled her gray-streaked, short brown hair. "Gage, I mean Detective Erikson, I really don't know what I can tell you about this mess. I kept to myself. Other than almost serving Blair nuts, my event was normal."

"I appreciate you staying to talk with me, Dora." I nodded to Peabody. "The detective is going to take notes. Is that okay with you?"

She glanced at Peabody and nodded as she focused her gaze on the floor. "That's fine."

"Can we talk about when you arrived yesterday morning? Did you notice anything? No matter how small or insignificant it might seem."

She twisted the hem of her sweatshirt around her fingers. "Let's see. When I arrived, I checked in and talked with Nancy Litchfield. You remember she was handling the registration. Once I was checked in, she told me where the coffee and tea were and to help myself. The three judges were huddled together, and not one of them had a smile on their faces. I told myself it would be a long event if they weren't even going to try and have fun. I mean, baking with cranberries can be delish, but it can also lead to a sour tummy. I took my spot in the baking center, set up my tools, and sat down to wait."

Leaning forward, I was intrigued by what could have been an argument between the judges. "Do you remember if the judges were drinking a beverage?"

She squinted her eyes. "I don't recall. But I was enjoying watching the others arrive. Other than Lily being new to the event, I've competed against the other finalists before."

"To your knowledge, did any other contestants have any run-ins with the judges prior to this event?"

With a wave of her hand, she laughed softly. "Frankie and Geoff always have a beef with one of them. They've never won the grand prize. Daisy had a crush on Roy, not that he'd ever notice her. He only had eyes for Blair. It's quite a tangled web in the baking world, you know."

I smiled as Dora's information included gossip, innuendo, and facts sprinkled together. "Is there anything else you can think of that might help us find out who harmed Roy Fletcher?"

She narrowed her eyes and screwed up her mouth to

one side. "Now that I think about it, Blair went and got three cups of coffee and gave each one a to-go mug."

Peabody shifted in her chair. "Then what happened?"

"The judges sat down, and Julian gave his opening speech." Dora looked from Peabody to me and asked, "Can I go home now? I'm tired; it's been a long weekend."

I pushed back the chair and stood. "Yes. If we need to speak with you again in the next few days, you'll come in."

"Gage, I want whoever did this caught." She covered her lips with her hand as if to stifle a sob. "Roy Fletcher was a lovely person and a fair judge. It's just not right that someone robbed him of a future."

Peabody escorted her out of the room and returned with Frankie Thorn.

"Mr. Thorn, this won't take long."

He scowled at Peabody. "The lady cop said I needed to bunk down at some motel for the night?"

"Correct. We're asking anyone who came to Pembroke Cove for the contest to stay a few days. Don't worry. It won't be at your expense. We must have a full picture of the events over the last two days."

He scraped a chair over the linoleum floor and sat down, crossing his arms. He slumped back in the chair and dropped his gray baseball cap on the table. "Yeah, I get it. Ask me anything you want, but you should realize, I pay very little attention to anyone when I'm baking. I get in the zone, as they say."

I nodded and ran through the same questions I had with Dora. This time, they yielded little new information. "Please leave your cell number with the desk clerk."

He stood. "You got it, and just so ya know. I hope you get the guy you did this to poor Roy. He was one of the good ones." He adjusted the cap on his head and strolled out the door. Peabody followed him out to bring Geoff in next. I sighed. After all my years of doing this, my gut told me I wouldn't learn anything new tonight. Not even from Daisy. She was going to need to sleep on things, and once she had some rest, she'd either come up with a better story or the truth would become clear.

Peabody walked in with Geoff Marks. He said, "I talked to Frankie about that motel. He's waiting for me to grab a bite to eat, and we plan on hanging around for as long as you need us. Roy was a great judge and a good man. This is just a darn shame." He plunked down in the chair, clasped his hands on the tabletop, and said, "Go ahead. Grill me. I've got nothing to hide."

I could see Peabody looking at me from the corner of my eye. After I ran through the same questions for a third time I still hadn't learned anything new.

When Peabody took Geoff out to the lobby, I followed her.

"Daisy, why don't you come on in?" I nodded in Julian and Blair's direction. "It won't be much longer."

Julian glared at me, and Blair studied the old magazine in her hand. *Field and Stream* did not seem to be her usual reading material. She lifted her eyes and met mine, then returned to the magazine.

Daisy walked two steps in front of me. "Detective Erikson, you know I did think of something."

I ushered her in the room. Peabody was waiting for us. I closed the door and double-checked the camera in the corner. The green record button was on.

"What did you remember, Daisy?"

She tapped the top of the table and looked at Peabody and me. Holding us captive with the tapping, she said, "Blair got Julian and Roy coffee right before we got started.

I'm not sure if you know this, but she uses the pink-packaged fake sugar. Roy was allergic to that. What if she put some in his coffee? I'll bet with the cream he never would have noticed the difference."

We were two for two, Blair got the coffee. "Did you see if she put aspartame into his cup?"

She shook her head. "No, but how else did it get in there?"

I wasn't about to tell her Roy could have ingested the substance in several ways, including before he arrived at the town hall. "That's what we have to discover." I leaned into my tried-and-true technique of giving my suspect a chance to talk.

Daisy dissolved into tears. "I can't believe it. I'm never going to be able to bake cookies for Roy. Did you know his favorite was oatmeal with dried cranberries and white chocolate chips?"

"Have you baked cookies for him before?"

She shook her head. "No. I just found out they were the only cookie he'd eat. Ironic. I should have made those for the contest, but apparently someone beat me to it."

I made a mental note. We needed to check to see if there was a tin of cookies in Roy's duffel bag.

Chapter 16
Lily

With a quick glance at Nikki, I turned my attention to the injured woman. "Nancy, what happened? Are you alright? Why didn't the ambulance take you to the hospital? What can we do to help?"

With the simple closing of her eyes, I guessed my rapid-fire questions were overwhelming.

She stepped away from the open door. "Come into the kitchen. I need to sit down." She made her way down the hall toward the back of the house, pausing at every table and door jamb to take a little break.

I put my hand under her elbow to steady her. With a grateful sigh escaping her lips, we covered the short distance.

Nikki had gone around us and pulled out a kitchen chair for Nancy to sit down. "Can I fix you some tea?"

"Thank you, Nikki. That would be lovely." She placed her folded hands on the black and white enamel tabletop. "I guess you can tell I've had better afternoons."

"Did you fall and hit your head?" Despite trying to slow

down and not pepper her with questions, I had several that needed answers. Especially if I was going to figure out if this was tied to what had happened to Roy.

It was obvious Nancy was in pain as she touched the bandage on her forehead and winced. Her voice shook as she said, "No. I got home from the contest and was getting my tote out of the trunk of my car. I was coming up the back walkway when someone clobbered me, wrenched the tote from my hand. I assume they ran away."

"Did you see who hit you? Or which way they went?"

She closed her eyes again and grimaced. "No. It happened so fast. I fell forward into the steps and must have blacked out for a couple of minutes. Once my head stopped swimming, I realized there was blood dripping off my face. You know, what they say about head wounds is true." She pointed to the floor near the back door. "I tracked it inside. I couldn't drive myself to the emergency room, so I called for help."

"Why didn't you let them take you to the hospital? You might need stitches, or you should be checked for a possible concussion."

"I'm fine. Really. They put a butterfly bandage on the cut. It turned out it wasn't that deep, and I said I'd clean myself up. But, of course, that nice Officer Jones said if I needed anything to call 911 and they'd send someone right over."

She refused medical assistance, and there was nothing to be done about that. I glanced around the room and noticed the smeared blood on the floor near the door, but thankfully, she hadn't tracked it any further. I patted her hand "I'm going to wipe up the floor while Nikki brews the tea. Just close your eyes and rest."

"Thank you, Lily. I'm so fortunate to have friends like

the two of you." She closed her eyes and rested her head on her arms atop the table.

I quirked a brow at Nikki. There were a few holes in her story, but I couldn't puzzle them out just yet. "Do you keep your cleaners under the sink?"

"Yes." Nancy didn't lift her head.

Nikki handed me paper towels and a spray bottle. The corner of her lip tipped up in a challenging smile. I glanced at the floor and remembered a spell that Milo had used to clean a chalkboard. All it took was a swish of his tail and a few words.

I looked at the mess on the floor and held my hand up vertically. Focused on the floor being cleaned I moved my hand from left to right while I said, "I wish it be." In a blink of my eye, the floor was pristine.

"Did you say something, Lily?" Nancy asked without lifting her head.

With a glance over my shoulder I said, "Almost finished." The tea kettle whistled, and I winked at Nikki. Saved by the stove. Then I noticed there wasn't a fire lit under the kettle. It was a good thing that she wasn't paying close attention to the two witches in her kitchen.

We sat at the table with mugs of steaming tea in front of us. Nancy clutched the mug between her hands. "Why did you stop by?"

"We're curious if you remembered anything about yesterday morning when Roy arrived."

She lifted the mug to her lips. "Like what?" Her breath rippled the surface of steaming tea. "The judges arrived around the same time. I showed them where to hang their jackets and the refreshment table. Then, I got busy with registrations. Even with it being a small event, it's important to have everything organized."

I scanned the tidy room. The only thing on her counter was a white and blue striped canvas bag. "That's very true, and you did an excellent job of keeping it running smoothly."

She tipped her head to the side and gave me a guarded smile. "Thank you. I try."

"Is there anything else you remember? The smallest detail might help crack this case wide open."

For several long seconds, she didn't answer me. Taking a tentative sip of her tea, she said, "I was a little hurt. Each judge had a white box of cookies waiting for them at their seat. Whoever left them didn't leave a box for me."

That piqued my interest. I leaned forward. "Were the cookies left anonymously?"

She nodded. "Each box had their names on the front. I overheard Blair saying they weren't tasty. I guess it was a good thing I was left out." A clock somewhere in the house chimed the hour. Nancy pushed her chair away from the table. "I don't mean to sound rude, but I'm feeling tired; I'd like to take a shower and get into comfy clothes. It's been an eventful day."

Taking her cue, Nikki and I stood. She put our tea mugs in the sink.

I said, "If there is anything you need, please don't hesitate to give me a call. I'm just a short distance away and can be here in a jiff."

"That's very nice of you. I'll be fine, except for a little headache, which will pass by the morning."

She escorted us to the door and ushered us out before firmly closing it. Standing on the porch, I scowled.

"Does it feel like we were rushed out of there, or was it just me?"

Nikki glanced over her shoulder as we heard the lock click into place. "I'd say we were dismissed."

I had the distinct feeling Nancy was watching us from behind the curtain. "Let's head over to the Clam Bake and pick up my order. I have a few things I want to jot down on my clue board while they're still fresh in my mind."

By the time Nikki and I reached my house, Gage's vintage cherry red pickup truck was in the driveway along with Sharon's motorcycle, which she'd drive until the first snow. Mac's truck, a car I didn't recognize, which I pegged as EL's, and Steve's Jeep, lined the sidewalk.

"It seems we're late to my dinner party." I pulled open the door and grabbed the brown cardboard box from the back seat. The decadent aroma of lobster bisque and garlic yeast rolls wafted on the breeze. My mouth watered as I carried the box into the kitchen.

Gage greeted me with a wide smile and a kiss on the cheek. He took the box from my hands and said, "We were finished a little sooner. I hope it's okay I had the gang come over early."

"This is great. After the last few days, being surrounded by friends and curious minds is perfect." I dropped my voice. "We stopped by Nancy Litchfield's before we went to the Clam Bake. As we were pulling up, an ambulance and police cruiser left. She claims to have been hit from behind and her tote bag stolen."

His brow arched. "Claims. I'm not sure I like where you're going."

"Yesterday, she had a white and blue striped bag at the registration desk. People tend to use the same tote for an extended period of time."

"Okay. You don't think it was stolen?"

I pressed my lips together and shook my head. "Nope. That tote bag was sitting on her counter, and that woman's tidy. There's no way she would have brought it home yesterday and left it sitting there."

"Are you saying you think she lied about being attacked?"

Nikki looked in our direction. "Hey, you two. If you're talking about Nancy, Lily should get her notes on the board so the group can dissect what we discovered."

Our friends were relaxing around the table. Gage placed his warm hand on the small of my back but didn't try to steer me to the other side of the kitchen. "She's right. I should get it all down."

"Dinner first. This way, your mind can whirl and churn over every detail." He brushed my cheek with his lips. "I know you, Lily Michaels. You need to mull things over first. The clue board can wait until after dinner."

I looked at Gage and then longingly at my clue board. My fingers itched to pick up the chalk, but it was better just to let everything gel in my brain. Something was niggling at me, but I couldn't quite put my finger on it. Food would be the catalyst for information going from brain to board. "Let's eat first and enjoy each other's company. This way, I can ruminate over the last few hours."

Everyone in the room agreed on food first and work second. I stepped aside as Mac and his wife Margaret offered to help get the rolls and bisque on the table.

"Mac, where's the baby?"

Margaret gave a shy smile. "You might find this awful, but when Mac called, I thought we could use this as a date night. It's been ages since we've done anything just the two of us. My mother-in-law agreed to watch her, and here we are."

I placed my hand over my heart. "Thanks for including us on your date."

Mac and Margaret chuckled, and she said, "Thanks for inviting us."

Sharon was with EL off to the side of the room. She twirled a lock of her dark hair around her finger while they chatted. I watched them for a moment, and realized they made a good-looking couple. Her dark eyes and hair complemented his blond curls and blue eyes. Steve was carrying the tray of lasagna to the table, and Gage was taking drink orders. I slipped away to the corner of the room, to where my clue board sat.

I double-checked to make sure everyone was busy as I jotted down a few things:

? White pastry box of cookies at each judge's chair. Nancy –
no
Tote bag? stolen or not
Daisy – Geoff Hospital?

I was lost in thought and didn't notice Gage until he was easing the chalk from my hand. "Sweetheart, dinner's ready, and there is plenty of time to write things down. Let's relax for the next hour and enjoy the mouth-watering lasagna Nikki whipped up."

I couldn't help but smile. "You're right."

The moment I felt Milo winding his body around my legs he said, "My dear witch, is it possible for me to have dinner? You wouldn't want me to wither away, and I have news, too. But there's no way I can put together coherent thoughts on an empty belly."

Gage picked him up, and I said, "Milo, if you're ready for dinner, I have a treat for you. While I was at Fred's place, I placed a special order. A nice piece of haddock. We can save the poached salmon Nikki prepared for tomorrow."

He pushed off from Gage's chest and looked me in the eye. "With seafood stuffing?"

Sharon laughed. "It seems that your fur baby knows the word haddock."

Gage placed him on a stool near the counter and not on his usual kitchen chair so I could unpack his dinner. "Sharon, I swear this cat is smarter than most people I know." Dropping a kiss between his ears I whispered, "And I mean that."

He tipped his head and looked me in the eyes. "Finally, you've discovered my secret."

Gage was watching us and winked.

"I'll fill you in later."

"Milo, enjoy your dinner," he said.

"Not to worry, Detective Cutie. I intend to."

I patted my overstuffed tummy as I eased away from the table. Dinner had been decadent, and Margaret had made a triple chocolate mousse cake for our dessert. I wasn't sure how I could stuff it in, but after we talked about the clues, I'd be ready.

"I have about as much energy right now as I would after Thanksgiving dinner."

Gage pushed back his chair. "The only thing missing is football on television."

"We have something more interesting to talk about.

Who killed Roy Fletcher? And welcome to Margaret and EL."

Sharon said, "For our newcomers, this is where Lily walks through clues she's discovered and offers ideas for us to follow up on."

With a quick glance at Nikki she gave me a knowing smile. These clues would help me help Gage and his team, and, with a little bit of luck, they'd be instrumental in solving the case.

I picked up a large piece of yellow chalk. "EL, you're a medical expert. Is it possible for Roy to have ingested cookies earlier in the day before they kicked in, causing him to collapse from a severe allergic reaction?"

His mouth dropped open, and he turned to Gage. "How does she do that?"

Gage shrugged his shoulders. "EL, she's just getting started. But you can answer the question since I see a note on the board about cookies."

"Lily. I. Um. Well. I can't provide details on this exact case, but yes, cookies, or any food, for that matter, would be slower to digest. It would take longer than drinking coffee laced with aspartame to be absorbed in the victim's system before causing a deadly reaction."

Snap. I knew it. "Before I talk about what may have happened to Roy, I'd like to share what Nikki and I uncovered this afternoon. When I'm done, whatever details you can share from questioning the suspects would be helpful."

Gage's facial expression never changed when I used the word suspects. Like me, he was reserving judgment. "Now, keep an open mind. Here is where things don't make sense. I'm fairly certain Nancy's not our main suspect, but something wonky is going on with her. According to her, when she got home today, she retrieved her tote bag from the trunk and then walked to the house when she was pushed from behind. Someone grabbed the tote and took off. However, she never mentioned closing the trunk before falling into the steps. I find that odd when she was so specific about the rest of the story." I held up my hand to fend off any questions. "Inside the kitchen, there was only blood in one spot. If she had come inside bleeding profusely, there would have been a trail of blood. Also, the tote she had yesterday at the contest was sitting on the counter. I didn't ask what color the tote was that she said was stolen or why someone would want it. And, the biggest flag, she hustled us out of her house as soon as she mentioned the boxes of cookies left for Roy, Julian, and Blair."

"Peabody? Did you secure the town hall this afternoon?" Gage asked.

"Yes, Detective. The scene will be untouched, so first thing tomorrow, I'll check for the containers of cookies and get them tested."

He gave her a warm smile. "When we're not at work, call me Gage, please."

She tipped her head and raised a brow.

Answering her unspoken question, he said, "Sharon, I'm sure."

I was happy to see how their relationship was morphing to a new, more personal level. "Now that we have that cleared up, can we return to the case?"

"Lily, this is great information, but you said you didn't think Nancy was the primary suspect? You're right about her timeline. Any chance you got a look at the car to see if the trunk was closed?"

"I did. When I volunteered to clean up the blood, I looked out the back door. The trunk was closed. In Nancy's defense, she could have left out details. We know she is upset with Julian and Blair, neither of whom had an aspartame allergy. If she was looking to make someone sick, all she had to do was use nuts or almond flour. That would have hurt the other two judges. Bottom line. Roy was the intended victim."

"Who did it?" Gage asked.

"Before I answer that question, tell me who left the police station before you had a chance to question them."

Mac and Sharon looked at each other. He asked, "How does she do that?"

I air high-fived Nikki. "Sharon, don't make me guess."

"Geoff and Frankie were both missing for a while. Geoff said he wasn't feeling well and needed some air. After he had been gone for a bit, Frankie volunteered to look for him."

"How long were they MIA?" I asked.

"About forty-five minutes."

Mac nodded, "Yeah, that sounds about right."

I drew circles around their names on the clue board. "Now we're making progress. What's next?"

Chapter 17
Lily

Gage tipped his head in my direction. "What idea is bubbling around your head, Lily?"

"The things we know for certain are that Julian, Blair, and Nancy have hard feelings about recipes. There is no judgment as to who did what to whom. Roy Fletcher was friends with them, and they all knew about his allergy. Contestants in baking competitions tend to be like groupies and follow them to participate, so with the exception of me, the other nine were all at least acquainted with all involved. Someone tried to kill Roy last night but was interrupted, Julian and Blair were seen at the hospital roughly two hours before the attempt."

Nikki asked, "Was there any security footage of the other suspects entering the hospital?"

I looked at Gage, Mac, and Sharon.

Mac said, "I scanned the footage and noted only hospital personnel entering and exiting the hospital with a three-hour window of the attempt on Mr. Fletcher's life."

EL looked around and opened his mouth and then closed it.

"Share your thoughts. This is an open conversation."

"I'd like to say this is cool, and don't mistake my comment, but Gage, is it normal to review a case with civilians?"

He chuckled. With a grand sweep of his arm, he said, "Allow me to introduce you to Pembroke Cove's version of Sherlock Holmes and Dr. Watson, also known as Lily and Nikki. Who goes with Lily to ensure she's safe and to be that extra set of eyes when needed."

Nikki beamed at Lily. "We make a good team."

"In addition, I learned a while back it was easier to have these informational get-togethers and talk about what Lily has discovered. It helps to keep her out of the line of danger."

Milo looked up from his spot sprawled across the back of the sofa and said, "Most of the time."

I glanced his way and gave him a stern look. Everyone, other than Nikki, heard him meow. She didn't react and hid a smile behind her hand.

"Milo." I attempted to keep my voice casual and convey a warning tone to keep comments like that to himself.

"Well, it's true. Whenever you've followed the clues in a murder case, you've ended up on the killer's radar."

There was no way I could respond and Milo knew it. I ignored him and focused on the clue board.

"Either the intruder was there before and found a clever hiding spot to wait until they could slip out, or he or she got out undetected."

Sharon said, "Mac and I will review the footage again tomorrow and expand the time after the attempt to the next shift change. Our perp has to be on camera at some point."

"If Sharon is going to investigate at the town hall, would it be okay if I went with her? I can run tests if we recover the cookies left for the judges. If they were made with a sugar substitute, at least, we could narrow down the delivery method of the allergen to Roy."

I asked, "EL, do you want to help us?"

He lifted one shoulder. "This might be an unorthodox investigation, but who am I to say it should be changed? If it's been working and all involved are good with it, I'd like to join in the quest."

It had been easy to convert EL to join us. "Perfect."

Gage jumped in. "Just for clarification, all reports come back through the proper channels. We must follow the custody of evidence. The last thing we'd need is to jeopardize an arrest."

"Good one, Detective Cutie. It's funny how he thinks you won't get your hands on every detail when you need it."

Ignoring Milo I said, "Nikki and I have never interfered with your investigation. What we uncover helps you arrest the real criminal."

He gave me a pointed look. I had seen that one before where he'd like to know what Milo was saying, but with our non-magical friends in the room, he couldn't ask. "Just as often, you end up on the wrong side of danger."

I gave him a sly wink. "That just speaks volumes about how talented I am at solving any puzzle."

Margaret held up her hand. "Can I ask a question?" Then she blushed and dropped it to her lap.

Mac clasped her hand in his. "Of course. What's on your mind?"

She scanned the group. Her cheeks were flushed a pale pink. "Is it possible Nancy faked the attack? Maybe she tripped while walking up her steps, and she fell and bumped her head. Lily said the tote bag she saw on the counter was the same one she had yesterday. I know I wouldn't have bothered changing bags in the midst of a busy weekend."

I nodded. "We agree. Mac, your wife might have a knack for solving murder."

He slipped a protective arm around her shoulders. "One investigator in the family is enough. I agree she has a way of seeing through a tangled mess to a logical assumption."

"I have to do that in my classroom every day with a group of sixth graders."

His smile was wide. "And your job is much harder than mine."

I had never seen this softer side of Mac. It was charming. With a quick glance in Sharon's direction, I noticed she was looking at her shoes. I surmised she was thinking how sweet the bond Mac and Margaret shared was. "I'm sure we all agree being a teacher is the most difficult as well as rewarding job, but friends, we need to focus on the case at hand."

Gage said, "I'll go see Nancy tomorrow and try to get some more details regarding who could have attacked her and why. I wonder how well she knows Frankie and Geoff. Could one or both of them be behind what she said happened?"

I puckered my lips. Drawing a line between Nancy, Julian, and Blair. I made three taps on the board with my fingertip. "My theory is Roy was the intended target. He was the only person on the panel who was allergic to aspartame. Blair and Julian have different allergies. An unknown person or persons wanted him out of the way to get a different judge on the panel, one who favored a contestant? Gage, after you're through chatting with Nancy, I'll run over there and talk with her about past baking competitions.

She might know if either Frankie or Geoff has been runner-up too often. We know Geoff thought I stole his spot in the cookie competition. Remember how Julian seemed to scoff at his entry, the oatmeal cranberry and chocolate combination?" When no one answered me, I said, "He wasn't kind at all. I felt bad for Geoff."

Nikki said, "Now that you mention it, I remember that too. I felt sorry for Geoff. Nobody deserves to be ridiculed like that, especially in public."

Mac's cell phone rang. He withdrew it and glanced at Margaret. "It's my mom." He got up and went into the kitchen.

I heard him say, "Okay, Mom, we'll be home shortly. Try not to worry." He came back to the living room with their coats in his hand. "The baby is running a fever. I'm sure she's teething but Mom wanted us to know. Lily, would you mind if we skipped out before coffee and cake?"

"Of course. Margaret, if you don't mind leaving your cake plate, I can drop it by tomorrow."

"No rush, Lily." Her face was pale and drawn tight as she pulled on her coat. "I'm sorry to leave in a rush, but the baby has never had a fever before."

I gave her a quick hug and reassured her that all would be fine. Gage walked Mac and Margaret outside. Nikki and Steve had relocated to the kitchen where she was plating dessert and he was making coffee.

EL and Sharon came in. I noticed he brushed her hand with his, and the smile that blossomed on her face made the evening end on a perfect note. Even if I hadn't had the opportunity to dig into the clues. Once everyone had gone home, Gage and I would walk through the photos I had taken and what information I had, plus a few other theories.

Gage came inside. His eyes twinkled as he noticed

Sharon with EL. He mouthed the word, *success* in my direction.

"Who's ready for dessert?" I asked.

Two hours later, I flopped on the corner of the sofa and propped my feet on the coffee table. My head was swimming. This vantage point gave me a clear view of the clue board and the photos. "Gage, what are we missing? I feel like the answer to who is the culprit is right in front of us."

He took my hand and brought it to his lips. "It usually is. Let's talk about our wedding. We're not ready to set the date yet, but do you want a big or small event?"

Pulling my legs under me, I turned to face him. "What would you like? It's not just my day; it's ours. I want it to reflect both our personalities."

"Nikki and Steve's wedding was a good size. It was casual with family and some close friends, and it was fun. Picking a day that most people wouldn't, St. Patrick's Day, was an interesting twist."

I couldn't help but smile. It was anything *but* a typical small wedding. "Except for the body in the bathroom, a destroyed wedding dress, pirate treasure, and that little brush with death. It *was* a perfect day."

"At the conclusion of all that mayhem, our best friends started the next chapter in their lives together. I'm looking forward to doing that as well. Which is why the wedding sets the tone for what comes next."

I was thrilled Gage wanted to be actively involved in the planning. "If I was to guess, you've put a lot of thought into how you see our day unfolding. Tell me, and then I'll share my ideas. Together, we can start the overall plan and refine things like the date down the road."

"I want Nikki to make not one but several cakes, all different flavor combinations. She's an amazing baker, and the carrot and browned butter cake they had at their wedding was the best I've ever eaten."

"Oh, and that cardamom buttercream frosting?" I did the chef kiss on my fingertips and said, "Pure perfection."

We laughed, and he said, "You've been hanging around Chef Julian too long." He gestured to the board. "We'll figure out who did this. But as always, I want you to be extra careful. Don't go off following a clue on your own."

I rolled my eyes. "I haven't done that in forever. Nikki or Milo always go with me."

"Lily." His voice was stern, and he looked me in the eye. "Promise."

"I don't go looking for trouble. Sometimes it knocks on my door. Literally."

He bobbed his head from side to side. "With all the excitement over the last few weeks, have you had time to work on any new spells from your book, *Practical Beginnings*?"

"Nothing complex. All I've done is bake."

Milo slunk into the room, jumped to my lap, and bumped Gage's hand for a pet. "What's Detective Cutie worried about?"

"He's wondering if I've been working on any new spells."

"Good, now he's my backup."

He purred as Gage scratched his ears. "What's Milo saying?"

"He's glad you're his ally in reading my book." I tapped the end of Milo's nose and said to Gage, "Do you remember seeing boxes of cookies on the judges' table when we arrived yesterday? I've been wracking my brain since Nancy mentioned them, and I don't recall seeing them." I sat up straight. "I know it's late, but what if we took a look tonight."

"Sweetheart. It's been a busy weekend and we're both tired. Don't you think it can wait until the morning?"

I shook my head. "No. I don't think so. Besides, I don't want a second-hand report. I'd like to see it with my own eyes."

Milo tipped his head back, encouraging Gage to scratch under his chin. In a contented kitty grumble, he said, "DC, you might as well cave and take her to the town hall. Otherwise, she'll make me go with her after you head home."

It was hard not to laugh since every word Milo said was true. "DC?"

He peered at me through squinted eyes. "A new nickname. Arrest me."

Gage's hazel eyes twinkled with merriment. "Care to clue me into this conversation between witch and familiar?"

Did I really want my fiancé to know that my familiar suggested I sneak into the town hall if necessary to look around before the sun came up? "Milo was saying he's up for an adventure tonight."

He groaned, threw his head back and stared at the ceiling. "All right. We'll go on one condition."

"Anything." I grinned, already thinking about checking every crevice of the old building in search of the puzzle pieces to Roy's death.

"We have to agree on the number of guests for our wedding and cakes with frosting flavors."

That was not what I had been expecting, but I was open to setting a few details in stone. "On one tiny condition, to your condition." I took his hand. "We keep this to ourselves.

Everyone wants to know the date, and I want us to choose a date that is special to us."

He leaned over Milo's head, who said, "Hey, watch it, dude." When Gage didn't move, Milo sank his claws on his leg as if he were kneading a blanket.

Gage pulled back and rubbed his leg. "Ouch, little man."

Milo hopped down, paused at the archway, and looked over his shoulder. "Let me know what time we're leaving," he said before stalking out of the room.

"Did I hurt him?"

I cupped his cheek in my hand. "Not in the least. He likes to make sure he's always taken into consideration first." With a feather-like kiss on his lips, I said, "Now, about our wedding. What if we had a beach-themed ceremony for our family and close friends. Then for the reception, we invite anyone who might want to come from town. We have so many friends and people who care about us it would be a shame to exclude anyone."

His brow had deep frown lines. "I like the idea. Doesn't that make it difficult to plan for food and drinks?"

I snapped my fingers and produced my wand. His eyes widened, and then he grinned.

"Magic, my love. We'll have never-ending food coolers and warmers. With all the witches in attendance, it will be easy."

"And for the cake?"

I tapped my temple. "I've got it. We'll need a big cake, so why couldn't we have each layer in the wedding cake be different flavors? This way, everyone can have what they like. Our special cake that we'll use for cutting and of course saving the top layer for our first anniversary could be a whipped cream and blueberry jam cake with maple butter-cream. Very Maine-like."

Gage drew me into his arms and looked deep into my eyes, causing the butterflies in my tummy to take flight. "And when might this extravaganza take place."

This man knew I had just come up with the perfect date for us to marry. "The Tuesday after Labor Day next September."

His face softened, his eyes grew moist. I watched as he tried to swallow the lump in his throat. "That was the day we first met in school. You're right. It is perfect." He wrapped his arms around me and held me close to his beating heart.

"And for now, our secret." I snuggled closer. Our search for clues could wait a few more minutes. I wanted to savor this moment with the man I had loved my entire life.

Chapter 18
Gage

I navigated the quiet Main Street. Storefronts were illuminated with security lighting.

"Gage, are you going to park in front of the town hall or behind the bookstore? Even if you don't park under a street light, darkness can't disguise your cherry red pick-up."

Lily's excitement was palpable. To her, searching for clues was as exciting as smoked salmon to Milo. "I thought I'd park at the station and we could walk down. But before we go, I'll let the desk officer know that we'll be there."

She nodded. "Right. Just in case a passerby reports a flashlight beam." She withdrew two small LED flashlights from her coat pocket.

I kept my face neutral, admiring how quickly she prepared for this late-night excursion. "Did you bring snacks, too?"

She frowned at me. "No. We can't drop any crumbs and contaminate the crime scene." Then her face softened. "Oh, I see that smile. You're teasing me."

I stretched my hand across the seat and clasped hers. "I love that you're focused on helping. This is a job for the department." She opened her mouth to talk, and I squeezed her hand. "But I'd rather be standing with you as you search for that clue that will make the pieces of this puzzle fall into place than have you go off on your own."

The corners of her mouth dipped. "Do you still think I can't take care of myself? You do realize how much I've grown in my skill as a witch over the last eighteen months."

The sad look, combined with her soft tone of voice, alerted me that I had hurt her feelings, which had not been my intention. "You're a very powerful witch. I've witnessed how hard you've worked on your craft. And I appreciate that you don't rely on your skills to make things happen. You're a combination of a witch and non-magical. All I ask is that you remember how much you mean to me. There could be a situation beyond your skill level, like a bullet, another witch, or I'm not sure what else. It calms me to know that I can be here with you tonight."

"It's not that I want to worry you when I poke around. To be clear, I love figuring out the clues, following where they lead, and challenging myself to think outside the box. It's just that, well, I have this burning need to stand up for the victims who can no longer speak for themselves."

I pulled into the station's parking lot and used my normal spot. Turning off the engine, I said, "I love that about you. Don't ever stop because I worry. All I ask is that you're careful."

"I promise. Unlike the first couple of cases I helped with, I understand desperation drives people to do bad things."

I was relieved and kept my voice light. "Do you have a plan for once we get in the town hall?"

"From the moment we walk in, I'm going to put myself in the footsteps of whoever the killer is. Walk through each step with fresh eyes. For this first scenario, they'll be bringing in the cookies. Since, as of this moment, that's the only logical way Roy could have ingested the substance. Once they're found and EL confirms they were sweetened with a sugar substitute, we will be closer to discovering how this tragedy unfolded."

She pushed open her door. The dome light bathed her lovely face in a soft, angelic glow. "Do you want me to come inside or wait for you out here?"

I got out, closed the door, and came around the back of the truck. Holding out my hand, I said, "Come inside. It's chilly out tonight."

We walked up the wide cement steps. Lily stopped when we reached the door. "We have come a long way. When Flora Gray was killed, you couldn't keep me far enough away from the crime scene."

I slipped an arm around her waist and pulled her close to me. "What's that old saying? If you can't beat 'em, join 'em."

She laughed softly. "At the Cozy Nook I'm sure I have a book with all kinds of standard phrases. I'll get you a copy."

"Just what I need: a guidebook of old but true sayings."

After I took the master key to the town hall from the police station, Lily and I hurried down the brick sidewalk past the bakery, hardware store, and the Copper Kettle. We paused at the front door. I withdrew the key. "Are you sure you want to do this tonight?"

"Yes, I need to see with my own eyes whether the box of cookies are still around and what else might have been missed."

I pulled two pairs of latex gloves from my pocket and

handed one to her. "Let's be careful not to disturb things, and feel free to take pictures."

She grinned. "I planned on it."

"I know. It was easier to be upfront than have you sneak them." The key turned easily in the lock. Like most older buildings in Maine, the exterior doors opened out to the street, with a vestibule and a set of interior doors. It was likely to keep cold air out as much as possible before central heat. A groan escaped the hinges as we entered the narrow room lit with security lights. I heard the snap of the gloves as Lily put hers on. She handed me a flashlight.

My heart quickened. A boost of adrenaline flooded my veins like it always did when I was about to investigate. "Ready?"

With a brisk nod, Lily said, "Affirmative." She turned on her flashlight and trained the beam on the floor. She walked around the perimeter of the space. Other than two empty black rectangular umbrella racks on either end of the room, there was nothing to see here.

I eased open the interior door, and we stepped into the main area, which was still set up as the baking center. Thankfully, nothing seemed to have changed since we left earlier today. The hallway leading to the town business offices were still roped off, and I made a mental note to check and make sure the offices were locked. To the left, restroom doors were ajar, and in the back, the small meeting rooms and storage areas would also need to be checked.

"Gage." Lily's voice was a loud whisper. She pointed in the direction of the ladies room. "I'll check in here if you want to check the men's room."

Speaking clearly and in my regular tone of voice, I said, "Sweetheart, there's no need to whisper. We're the only ones here."

She gave me a thumbs-up. "Got it," and disappeared into the restroom. Before I followed her lead I flicked on the overhead lights. We had nothing to hide. This was official police business even with a civilian present.

The restroom garbage can was empty. It was obvious the bathroom had been cleaned. Hopefully Jonesy had collected the garbage and taken it to the station. If there had been anything in here we had the evidence. When I came out Lily was walking down a row of chairs, the flashlight beam circled around the base of each seat. She methodically made her way up and down the first two rows before she caught me watching her.

"What are you looking for?"

"Anything? Something? I figured I'd start here with low expectations and move on to the more exciting areas."

She was working her process. Gathering details that might have been overlooked.

"Gage, why didn't you secure the scene yesterday when Roy collapsed or even this morning?"

I wondered when she'd come up with this question. "Yesterday could have easily been an accident. We had no reason to believe Roy was targeted for any reason. It wasn't until I learned about the attempt on his life that I had to make a tough decision. Cancel the event or bring everyone who was a suspect back to see how they interacted. With some luck, I would see how they'd respond to the news about Roy."

She continued to scan the floor and chairs methodically. "Oh, keeping everyone under one roof on the guise that they're not suspects. Brilliant."

"I can't take credit for the idea. It's a procedure that works."

She finished with the rows of chairs and moved in the

direction of the registration desk. With one foot on the riser, she turned her head in the direction of the offices. "Did you hear that?"

I paused, opening the oven at Dora's baking center. I heard the whistle of the wind under the eaves and a rustle of leaves skittered over the window panes. "It's just the wind."

Seeming to hesitate, her body posture rigid. "Maybe I should cast a protection spell."

"We're fine. Besides, who's going to burst in here at this time of night?"

"Whoever killed Roy might want to snag a piece of evidence that could lead back to him or her." She shook her head. "What happened to thinking like the bad guy."

I pointed to the registration desk. "Check out the space over there. I'll continue here."

With an impatient huff, she held the beam of light under the table and then moved around the backside. Pushing aside some papers, she said, "Gage, come look at this."

"You found something?"

"Yes. You're going to need an evidence bag."

I hurried through the baking center and reached her side to see what her flashlight trained on. "Is that a threatening note?"

You missed your chance at greatness. Settle for mediocrity. It's all you're worth.

Lily glanced my way after she finished reading it. "Are you thinking what I am?"

"Yeah. This note could apply to almost anyone involved. Julian, Nancy, Blair, Geoff, even Frankie."

"Remember, Daisy and Dora, if we want to round out the entire list. I still say Dora has nothing to do with it, but she's the only one. Daisy claims to be in love with Roy. Julian and Blair have their own personal battle waging. Now Nancy is tossed in, but I can't see her wanting to hurt Roy. Geoff and Frankie disappeared during questioning around the same time Nancy was attacked."

"Supposedly attacked. We don't have anyone to corroborate her story. You said yourself the tote she used yesterday was on the counter."

Lily tapped the tabletop. "This proves there was a threat. Roy had to have been involved somehow. I just can't figure it out."

After Lily took a picture of the note, I slipped it into an evidence bag. She finished looking at the papers on the clipboard before setting it aside.

"Anything of interest?"

"Nancy kept score during each segment as if she were a judge. But she didn't taste the food, so her score was based on the appetizing look and presentation of the sweets."

"Why wasn't she a judge? She's a talented baker who also went to school with Julian and Blair. Instead, they chose Roy."

"We talked about that yesterday during registration, and because she helped with the pie recipe, she disqualified herself."

I rolled my shoulders and neck. "The pie that Julian accused you of stealing from his cookbook. My guess is he thought you'd try to impress him and sway his vote."

"There is some discrepancy on that point. Remember, Nancy said it was her recipe." She crossed her arms over her chest and frowned. "And in my defense, I elevated it with the sugar cookie crust, taking the basic pie and making it sublime. And for the record I didn't know Blair had a signature snickerdoodle."

I loved seeing her confidence blossom even if she was annoyed in this moment. "Which is why you won."

"Back to the note. If it was among Nancy's papers, it must have been something she received. If you think about it, Julian helped destroy her reputation, so the note makes sense." She moved to the judges' table. It was as littered today as it had been yesterday with the exception of Fred's seat. His space was neat and tidy. Lily withdrew a small square trash can from under the table.

"Gage." Her voice went up an octave. "Jackpot." She glanced my way, her eyes bright. "I found a white pastry box."

"Take pictures before you remove it from the garbage can."

Lily had her cell phone out. She was moving around the table taking a lot of pictures. Then she placed the box on the tabletop. Roy Fletcher was scrawled across the top. She took a few more before she eased open the lid. Inside. Cookies. There looked to be a couple of varieties. "There isn't any oatmeal, white chocolate chip."

Her voice filled with disappointment at her discovery. "I would have guessed there would be several of them in the box. They were Roy's favorite per Nancy."

"We need to find the other two boxes." I pulled out the next chair, looking for the garbage can. But it was empty. "Did you say she also said Blair was disappointed in them? Maybe she didn't finish any and we'll have a better idea of what was in the box that Roy could have eaten."

She pulled out the chair where Julian had sat. "It's not here either." Scanning the room, she focused on the baking shelves. "This way."

I followed her as she moved quickly.

"Over there. Pastry boxes are on the corner shelf." She pointed to a short stack of three.

I held up the flashlights as she pulled them from the shelf, which swayed from side to side. I put out a steadying hand, and when it was stable again, I saw Chef Julian scrawled across the top of the box. I set that one aside on the counter. On the next box was Blair Holt, whose name could be on the third.

Lily took the second box off and read it out loud. "Nancy Litchfield."

Chapter 19
Lily

I snapped a bunch of pictures before talking out loud, "We have four boxes of cookies." I looked at the variety in each box, and Roy's was the only one without the oatmeal variety. Sugar cookies, brownies, and dark chocolate chip cookies were neatly stacked inside. "Do you think these came from Blair's bakery?" I picked up one of the boxes and looked at the underside. "There's a nut-free sticker."

Gage said, "That box could be meant for Blair."

"No. It's labeled Nancy. But Julian told me that Blair's bakeshops promote being completely nut-free in all locations. This protects her and alleviates the fear of cross-contamination. I did a little research last night. Nut allergies are pretty common, and fifty percent of the time, a reaction can present later in life."

"And that's what happened to Blair?"

"From what Julian said." I drummed the top of the pastry box. "We need to talk to Blair and see which cookie she tasted and didn't like."

"Why?"

"What if, and stay with me for a minute, she tried the same cookie as Roy? She's a professional baker, so the sugar substitute would taste off to her. But that was the baker's intent. EL will need to test each cookie from each box to see which ones were baked with sugar or aspartame."

"That's tomorrow's experiment after we've had some sleep. We'll secure the room and take the rest of the night off." Gage said, "I can't think clearly anymore tonight."

The sound of glass breaking stopped me dead. "You had to hear that."

Gage pointed in the direction of the offices. "Someone's back there." He eased around the table, and his hand automatically went to his side, where his holster normally sat. But we'd come from my house, and he wasn't armed. But I was just in a different way.

I pointed to our feet and whispered, "Silence is golden, even for feet. For this, I wish so it shall be." It was not very poetic, but once the words had been said, the sounds our shoes made on the wood floor evaporated.

Gage didn't look over his shoulder but did give me a thumbs-up. We walked slowly in the direction of the thick rope that was draped from one side to the other. Slipping underneath it, Gage hugged the wall. I followed suit. My heart was hammering in my chest. Who was trying to break into the town hall at this time of night? Before we reached the first door, Gage stretched out his hand to stop me. He put a finger across his lips, pointed to himself, and then to the door.

I knew he was indicating he was going in. I wasn't about to let him go alone. I placed my hand on his arm. This time I didn't speak the words but closed my eyes and concentrated power from deep within me. *"From the depth of my soul to the recesses of my brain. I wrap Gage in the protection of my love."* The energy pulsed from my body, and I could feel the protection spell wrapping around him. I gave a nod that it was safe for him to move forward.

The amulet I wore under my shirt warmed against my skin. There was danger ahead. I thanked the stars for the warning and itched to burst through the door and stop whoever was on the other side.

Gage reached his hand to the doorknob when it turned. Whoever was in the office was coming out.

I yanked on his arm and jumped back. We needed to get back down the hall and hide around the corner until we knew who we were dealing with. The element of surprise was critical.

With our footsteps silent, it was easy to run to the rope, duck under, and get out of sight before they came out. It seemed like time crawled, but we made it as the door creaked open. Whoever it was, they were extremely cautious.

Beads of sweat prickled the back of my shirt. Gage was like a statue, but I knew he was alert to every slight move-ment the perp was making. He pointed to his eyes and then down the hall. Another crash came from behind us, and I nearly jumped out of my skin. I managed to contain the scream that bubbled up. It was the shelf that had swayed just a few minutes ago. I stared in that direction but didn't see anyone who could have knocked it over. Was it possible a witch was inside the building? Was I prepared to battle against someone who meant to do harm?

My fingers itched to hold my wand, and I silently admonished myself. I should never have left home without it. How can I help Gage if I wasn't fully prepared? One of us should be. I shifted focus from the baking center to the muffled sounds of a person creeping in our direction. I pressed against the wall so as not to cast a shadow on the floor.

I clasped my amulet, and to my surprise, it was now cool to the touch. That was odd. It should be burning up. Milo's voice echoed in my head. *Trust your instincts, or there could be dire consequences.*

A calmness stole over me. Whoever was coming down the hall wasn't a foe. I had no way to convey this message to Gage before he sprang, tackling the person as they came around the corner.

A grunt and then a groan, "Get off me," came from under the impressive tackle Gage had launched.

"Julian?" I took a step forward. "What are you doing here?"

Gage hauled the chubby chef to a standing position. "And why did you break a window to get in."

He held up his hands in surrender. "I didn't, honest. If you don't believe me, go take a look at the office I was in. The window is fine. In fact, when I heard the glass break, I came out to investigate."

Gage frowned. "Keep an eye on him. I'm going to check out the offices."

I nodded. "We'll be fine."

Julian rubbed the back of his head where it connected with Gage and grimaced. "Your boyfriend must have been a football player. He landed that tackle like a pro."

Walking around Julian, I had a better vantage point to watch Gage as he made his way down the hall to check each office. He inserted a key into the second door and eased it open. Light flooded the hallway behind him. I could picture him walking around the room, checking under the desk and other possible hiding spots. A few minutes later, he returned and repeated the same procedure for each office. Finally, he strode in my direction, his lips thinned and unsmiling.

"You didn't find anything?"

He shook his head. "I'm going to check the rest of the building," he said, bobbing his head in Julian's direction.

I lifted a shoulder and let it drop. "Be careful."

"You too."

"Hey," Julian shouted after Gage. "I'm a chef. Do you think I'd risk my hands hurting someone?"

"You never know what motivates people. If pushed far enough, anyone could react with poor judgment." Pointing to a chair near the baking center, I said, "How about you take a seat? When Gage is done, we'll figure out where to go from here."

He got on his hands and knees and pushed to his feet. Grabbing the back of the chair, he again rubbed his head. "I might have to bring charges against him. He assaulted me."

I narrowed my eyes. "Think very carefully about that. You were breaking into a town building at night, creeping up on an officer in the midst of conducting a homicide investigation. Somehow, I don't think you'd be successful."

He dropped his chin to his chest. "This is about Roy?"

I slapped my hand to my thigh. "What did you think we were doing here in the middle of the night? Revisiting recipes?"

He withdrew a slip of paper from his jacket pocket and handed it to me. "This note was slipped under my motel door."

Still wearing my gloves, I took it and read:

If you want the truth, come to the town hall at one a.m. Alone!

"Let me guess. You have no idea who left this but decided to play amateur sleuth to find out?"

He lifted his head, his fleshy chin wobbling. "If coming down here in the middle of the night gave me peace of mind, I was going to do it. I still can't believe he's gone. How could anyone have wanted to hurt Roy? He was a gentle soul. His only failing was his weakness for oatmeal cookies. I mean, if you have to have one cookie to eat, make it something utterly delicious. Like a shortbread infused with other flavors. Poetry of simple ingredients blending to make the perfect cookie."

Pointing to his chest, I said, "Stay put." I crossed the room to where the boxes of cookies sat. I flicked open the box with Julian's name on it and saw it contained shortbread. "What is Blair's favorite cookie?"

His brow crinkled. "Chocolate, white chocolate chip. She calls it Pure Decadence. It's also in my first cookbook."

I tipped my head. "Really. Maybe there's truth to what she said about you publishing her recipes as your own?"

He held out his hands, palms upward. "She's already extracted a pound of flesh, or should I say a small fortune from my royalties."

"I looked in the box labeled Blair Holt. It contained a chocolate cookie that wasn't in the others. "Do you happen to know Nancy's cookie of choice?"

His forehead wrinkled. "Back when we were in culinary school she loved my snickerdoodles. And before you ask, that was my recipe or really my granny's."

This was odd. Snickerdoodles were in the box labeled Nancy, and the shortbread and chocolate cookies were in

Julian and Blair's boxes, respectively. Was I jumping to the conclusion that Roy's box had the oatmeal cookies he loved? If yes, then each box was specific to the recipient. Or was that a diversion too? My head ached with questions I wished I had the answers for. I swiped a clipboard with a pad of paper from the sideboard and a pen, and strode over to where Julian was sitting. Thrusting it out, I said, "I'd like for you to write the following, each name on its own line. And write so I can read it." I tapped the page. "Start with your name. Followed by Blair, Roy, and then Nancy. First and last names."

Julian squinted as he looked at me. "You want me to write everyone's names on this paper? Printing or cursive?"

"Print please." That was the last of the directions I was going to give him. If my hunch paid off, I could clear Julian of making the cookie boxes.

After about a minute, Julian handed me the clipboard. I then walked over to the judges' table and picked up his discarded scoring sheet. Taking both of them I went to the boxes. I wasn't a handwriting expert, but everything matched the score sheet and the clipboard. However, there were very different curves on the a's and o's on the boxes. I set all the samples together and tore off a piece of paper.

EL, check the shortbread for almond flour and the chocolate cookies for traces of nuts.

Gage was coming out of the storage room. "All clear. When it's daylight I'll have an officer check to see if they can find any broken glass on the ground."

I crooked a finger in his direction. "You need to call EL and he needs to do the analysis tonight. I don't think you'll want to wait after you take a look at this. If my hypothesis is correct I know who doctored the cookies for all three judges and not just Roy's."

"What are you talking about?" He scanned the three writing samples and looked at me. His eyes grew wide. He spoke loud enough for me to hear him. "Are you saying that Julian wasn't responsible?"

"Correct. If we have the shortbread in Julian's box tested we'll find it was made with almond flour, the chocolate cookies contain nuts, just like the oatmeal cookies would have contained aspartame." I grabbed his arm and squeezed. "This wasn't about any one judge in particular it was about getting rid of one to shift the balance to a neutral party."

He took a step back. "Do you think it was Nancy?"

With a thrust of my chin, I never blinked. "No. I've narrowed it down to one of the contestants. Tomorrow morning, we're going to bring them all here, along with Sharon and Mac, and you'll be able to arrest the guilty party."

"Lily... you have narrowed it down though. I can tell by that steely glint in your eyes."

I tapped the edge of his cell phone sticking out from his shirt pocket. "Call the team. We need everyone here to get ready."

Gage looked across the room to where Julian was slumped in the chair. "What about him? Do we let him go back to the motel or stay here?"

I didn't need to look at the chef. He was an empty soul, hurting at the loss of his friend. "He needs to answer a few more questions before everyone arrives."

Gage handed me his phone. "Will you text my detectives? I have to get answers to your questions." He winked at me and then said, "Julian." His voice held the authoritative tone of a detective.

He snapped his head up, body straight in the chair. "What did I do?"

"Entered a town building after hours. I want to know how and why, so start talking."

Gage pulled up a chair next to Julian and sat down. I quickly jotted off a group text to Sharon, Mac, and EL, asking them to come to the town hall. There was no need to wait for a response they'd be here soon. I leaned against the counter, alert to questions Gage would pose to Julian.

"Why do you want to shut down Blair's bakeries?"

That was not the line of questioning I had expected, but it was a good start. Their animosity had run high for the last two days.

"I don't." Julian shifted in his chair. "I've always wanted Blair to succeed. The rats, that wasn't me. Honestly, I'm telling the truth. Did I borrow her recipes? Sure, but I've paid for that. My publisher dropped me. I'll never be able to release another cookbook on my own again. The only way I could is to work with Blair, and I've been trying to convince her to forgive me."

"You're not out to destroy her business?"

He glanced from me to Gage. "No. Never. When I heard about the trouble I started asking questions. I still don't have any idea who did." He glanced at the floor.

Gage leveled his gaze at Julian. "You have an idea. A former schoolmate? Another judge?"

He shook his head. "Roy, Blair, and I were great friends. We had fun doing these events together."

"What about Nancy?"

"She might hold a grudge. Her leaving school had less to

do with us and more with her skill. As a baker, she's above average, but Nancy didn't have the chops to become world-class in a kitchen. I'm not trying to sound mean. She dropped out because she couldn't cut it. Plain and simple. Maybe Nancy was frustrated that she wasn't asked to be a judge." His eyes grew wide, and he snapped his fingers. "Wait. She knows our favorites and bakes a great cookie. Do you think she was the one who poisoned Roy and ultimately killed him?"

Lily

Julian was slumped over the table, snoring after Gage had grilled him. But he'd stuck to his theory that Nancy must have been the one to bake the cookies and subsequently kill Roy. That didn't jibe with me. Nancy was also supposed to get cookies, and her box contained snickerdoodles, but the allergen, if there was one, was unknown at this point.

Sharon and Mac combed the room again for clues. EL picked up the pastry boxes to analyze all the cookies. Without knowing exactly what Roy had eaten, we were going to have to take a leap of faith and test the remaining cookies in the other boxes. With a bit of luck, soon, we'd know about all of the varieties.

I called Nikki. "Hi there, any chance you could do me a favor?" I knew it was early but she was always up before the sun.

"Anything."

"I need to see my clue board, and with all the non-magicals around, it's not easy for me to magick it here. Could you pop over to my place, snap a couple of pictures, and text them to me?"

"Give me five minutes." She clicked off.

I could feel the frown taking up permanent residence on my face. This puzzle was not coming together like the other investigations I had been a part of, which was somewhat disappointing. I thought I knew what to expect. I, too, was focused on Nancy; the others were becoming less likely to have been the murderer. Each box had been prepared specifically for an individual or, should I think, a potential victim.

Gage sat with Julian, who stared at his clasped hands. I kept looking at the notes on my clue board. Frankie and Geoff had disappeared yesterday. Where had they been? I glanced at the time and jumped to my feet. With energy to burn, I pointed to the front door and mouthed, "Coffee?"

Gage smiled and nodded. I knew how Sharon and Mac took their coffee, so I asked Julian.

"Just cream. Thanks." I wanted to confirm from what he had said yesterday.

The early morning air was fresh and clean. I coughed as I inhaled the freezing air deeply into my lungs. I pulled the collar of my jacket around my neck, wishing I had brought my scarf. I looked around to see if there were witnesses, but the coast was clear. I closed my eyes and, under my breath, said, "The bitter cold I can not stand when the warmth of a scarf can be at hand. For this I wish, so it shall be, produce a scarf made just for me."

In the time it took me to exhale, a pale pink cashmere scarf draped around my neck. It matched my cranberry-colored jacket. I readjusted it and jogged down the stone steps. When I reached the bottom, I continued my light jog in the direction of the Sweet Spot bakery. If nothing else, I might burn off the pent-up energy. If my thoughts would clear, I could go back to the town hall with fresh eyes.

Clues about this case tumbled around my brain. The biggest unknown was Nancy Litchfield. William knew almost everyone in town. He'd know what happened regarding culinary school, and I might be able to glean who could have had a grudge against her. The puzzle pieces were mounting up, and by the end of the day, if she were the strongest suspect, Gage would make an arrest.

I pulled open the door to the bakery, and my forward motion stopped. All of my suspects but one were sharing a table, a carafe of coffee, and a plate of muffins— Nancy, Geoff, Frankie, Daisy, and Dora. Blair was the only one missing.

Conversation died. Each person looked anywhere but at me.

"Good morning," I said, trying my best to have a bright and cheery outlook. I could see William from the corner of my eye, watching the scene unfold. I flashed him a smile. "Can you ring me up for six coffees and I'll need a tray, please?"

"Sure thing, Lily. Anything else to go with it?"

"No, thank you." I strolled over to the table littered with sugar granules, coffee drips, and crumbs. "How's everyone this morning?"

Nancy gave me a side eye before staring at the coffee mug clutched between her hands. She now sported a small one-inch round bandage over where she had cut her head. "It's just great. I'm waiting to be hauled into the police station for more questions."

Without looking up, Dora added, "Roy's only fault was eating too many oatmeal cookies."

Daisy nodded, "Sad."

Geoff leaned back in his chair and looked at me; his upper lip curled in a sneer. "Too bad he died before the contest was over. I'm sure there would have been a different outcome."

I didn't rise to the bait of that comment, but I felt the need to defend Fred's honor. "There were three judges on the panel, not one. The contest was fair."

Frankie snorted and focused his attention out the window. "You go on and think that."

"Has anyone seen Blair this morning?"

Nancy drained her coffee and smacked the mug against the table. "Nope, and I don't care. She and Julian are probably packing up to get out of town before the next shoe drops."

"Lily," William called to me, "your order's ready."

My cell vibrated with an incoming message. After reading it I sent Gage a text.

All the suspects are together except Blair. Have them come to the town hall. I've figured out who killed Roy and why.

I gave William a sweet smile and flipped my head a fraction of an inch over my shoulder to the suspect table. I gave a slight wink "Wait for it."

Ping, ping. Their phones all chimed simultaneously.

After giving William a few bills, I said, "Group texts. You gotta love them." I folded back the tab on one of the coffees and took a mind-alerting sip before picking up the tray with the remaining five. "It's time to put this case to bed. But can I make a request?"

"Of course."

I leaned closer to the counter. "Any chance there will be cinnamon pecan rolls with extra icing later today?"

He chuckled. "I think that can be arranged. As long as you don't ask for Lulu's secret recipe."

I held up both hands. "No worries there. I have all the recipes I need, and for any other baked goods, I have you and Nikki." Over my shoulder, I could see the baking contestants filing out of the shop. "See you later." I sipped my coffee again and was ready to help Gage and the department put a lid on the case.

The sun seemed a little brighter on my return trip and I took that as an encouraging sign. As I approached the building, EL was standing by the front door.

"Hold up, EL."

He met me halfway down the steps and held out his hand to take the drink tray. "I got a text from Gage. He said everyone was meeting, and if I had any information about the cookies, I should join the party."

"Since you're here, I'm guessing you do."

"You got that right. Care to guess?"

The twinkle in his eye made me think of a genius at work or a mad scientist. Either way, he was one of us, or as I thought of our little group, the good guys.

"There were oatmeal cookies in one of the trash bins, which you're guessing were from Roy's box? They were made with sugar substitute. Blair's cookies contained ground nut powder. Julian's shortbread was made with almond flour, and Nancy's snickerdoodles were perfectly fine." I gave him a wide grin. "How'd I do?"

His eyes widened before returning to normal. "All true. How do you do that? Cut through the noise and ferret out the answer?"

"Today, fresh air, a walk and William's coffee."

He tipped his head as he studied my face. "You know who baked them too, don't you?"

Nodding, I said, "I believe so, but now it's show time. Would you like to stick around after you deliver the official report to Gage?"

"Just try to get rid of me." He walked the last steps next to me and pulled open the exterior and interior doors.

As we entered the room, shouting and chaos ensued. Gage put his fingers to his lips and a shrill whistle cut through the noise.

"Everyone, be quiet." He pointed to chairs in a semicircle. Blair and Julian were already seated. Sharon and Mac stood behind them. He acknowledged EL and me with a brisk nod and waved us forward.

As I thought, Blair was in town, just not hanging out with the others. I passed the tray of coffee to Sharon. Now was the perfect time to get a good jolt of caffeine, and what was about to happen would be enough to excite me.

Gage paced in front of the judges, sans Fred Wickshire, Nancy, and the four final contestants. "Listen up. This is a bit unorthodox, but it's time the killer is exposed. Someone left the original panel of judges boxes of cookies." He glanced at Nancy, "Including you."

She placed her hand on her heart as her mouth formed a large O. "I wasn't forgotten?"

"Trust me, you didn't want to be on that list." He extended his hand for the report EL held in his. He scanned the notes. His lips curled back in a grim smile as he stepped away from the seven people watching his every move. "EL, you're sure?"

"Yes, Detective Erikson."

Our suspects looked at each other. It suddenly dawned on them that a killer was in their midst.

Geoff said, "I know my rights. I want to call a lawyer."

Gage splayed his hands, palm side up. "You haven't been arrested. Yet."

Geoff's face drained of color. He seemed to shrink into the chair as if he wanted to disappear.

With a sweep of his arm in the direction of the now-silent suspects, Gage said, "Lily, would you care to share your insights into this case?"

I pressed my hand over my amulet. It was slightly warm against my skin. If this went sideways, I could react faster with witchcraft than Sharon or Mac with their weapons. Based on my amulet, Roy's killer was only a mild threat at the moment. And as Milo had reminded me to trust my instincts.

Standing front and center, I took a moment to really look at each person. Did anyone flinch? Was their body language screaming guilt or innocence? It didn't matter. I took a deep breath and exhaled.

"I know who the killer is. I think I know why. I definitely know how." I paused for dramatic effect. Dang. Not a single flinch. I had expected more.

"Two days ago, Roy, Blair, and Julian each had a white pastry box of cookies with their names on the top sitting on the judges' table." I gave a pointed look at Nancy. "We discovered one on the shelf in the back with your name."

She sat up a little straighter and looked at the others with a smug smile as if this was a proud moment in her life to be included.

I crossed my fingers behind my back as I was about to fib. But it was to smoke out the guilty. "Roy's box contained several kinds of cookies, including oatmeal cranberry, his favorite. Blair's Chocolate-chocolate chip, Julian's contained shortbread, and Nancy's had snickerdoodles. All your favorites. What you didn't know is that each one of them was made with a secret ingredient. Roy's had sugar substitute, Blair's had a powdered nut, Julian's almond flour, and Nancy's weren't tainted."

Nancy's eyes bulged and her face froze in a look of horror. She managed to sputter out, "I didn't make those cookies."

I cocked a brow and scanned the row of people. Walking from left to right, the heels of my boots clicking against the wood floor. With each step, Frankie's shoulders curled forward, and he cast a look in Geoff's direction, who kept his eyes glued to the wooden floor. Daisy and Dora sat like a cement statute.

Blair said, "You're saying that any one of us could have met that same fate as Roy?"

"Except Julian. He tells everyone he's allergic to almond flour, but he's not." I gave him a pointed look. "Correct?"

Dora folded her arms over her chest. "What do you mean he's not allergic?"

"Occasionally, people don't tell the full truth, do they, Dora?" Daisy asked.

"Stay out of this, Daisy." Dora glared at the woman. "Your baked goods are average. If it weren't for Roy, you'd have been drummed out of all events long ago. Everyone knew he was secretly smitten with you, which is why he kept voting for you."

"That's not true. We didn't have that kind of a relationship. I mean, I liked him, but he kept me at arm's length, including the night I went to dinner when he was in town. He didn't even want me at his table." She sniffed and wiped her cheeks with the back of her hand.

Blair leaned forward in her chair. "Daisy, get a clue. You

were chasing him, and he had no idea how to handle it. He kept you in the friend zone for a reason."

Dora got to her feet, slamming her chair into the baking center. "I'm leaving."

I nodded to Sharon and Mac. They stepped in Dora's direction. "Before you do, why don't you tell us why you wanted to get rid of Roy?"

She tipped her head back, and her laugh was tinged with malice. "I didn't mean for him actually to die. I needed new judges. I figured if he got sick, they'd put Nancy in his place." She nodded in the shocked woman's direction. "We've been friends for years, and she'd support me and maybe even convince these other pompous jerks to go along with her. At one time, they had been the three musketeers until greed and petty bickering got in their way. I figured that, too, could work in my favor." Tears spilled down her cheeks. "And I'm sorry about pushing you down. I waited to make sure you got up before I left."

Nancy drew her head back. "Why did you want to hurt me? Like you said, we've been friends for a long time."

I asked, "Dora, were you trying to redirect any suspicion that might fall in her direction?"

She nodded. "When Nancy was groggy, I put her tote bag on the counter, too. I'd never steal from her. Then I waited until she got up before I left."

At least that wrapped up that tiny puzzle. I took a step in her direction. It would be easier to cast a wide protection spell around the others if I could pull her away from them. Not that I thought she had a weapon with her. "Did you mean to kill Roy with the pillow?"

She wrinkled her nose and scuffed the floor with the toe of her shoe. "Well, it seemed like a good idea at the time. You know, who'd suspect 'lil ole me? The oldest and most frail of the bunch. Besides, I saw Daisy and Geoff hanging around. I was sure that would get mentioned at some point." She lifted one shoulder and shrugged. "When someone's in a coma, they can't fight back. I didn't count on that stupid nurse coming in to check on her patient."

"And the EpiPens?"

She grinned. "A quick thought. I knew Roy had one in his coat pocket and when I saw Blair pull one from her jacket I knew I could brush up against her and grab them both. No meds, no quick rescue."

This woman was cold. "What was your motivation to do this?" I took another step closer as Sharon and Mac did the same. I could feel Gage ready to spring into action, too.

"I'm moving to Florida to live in a retirement village. The cold has gotten the best of me. I leave next Monday. All I wanted was to win. This is my last baking event and winning the cranberries competition doesn't make me a criminal."

Gage nodded to Sharon. She withdrew handcuffs from her belt. "No but poisoning people does."

I said, "Dora Ingalls, you're about to be under arrest for killing Roy Fletcher, and the only move you'll be making is to jail."

Epilogue

I arrived at the Cozy Nook mid-morning. I unlocked the door with a flick of my wrist and stepped inside the sunny space. Milo was waiting for me on his normal window cushion.

"My dear witch," he hopped down from his perch and padded across the floor and jumped into my arms. "Hello, little man."

"The bad guy has been arrested?"

"Bad woman, and yes, she's been charged with Roy's death and probably a few other charges of aggravated assault at least."

Milo pulled back. "What are you saying?"

"Dora doctored up cookies for the judges, a special flavor that each one liked with a substance they were allergic to. Thankfully, Roy was the only one who ate them, and that's sad too because he didn't make it and she gave herself away at the bakery."

"How?

"Dora slipped and said that Roy ate too many oatmeal cookies. At that point, no one knew about that connection."

He butted my chin with his little head. "Does this mean, with the baking thing behind us, we can go back to normal?"

I laughed softly. "Only you would call being a witch with a talking familiar normal."

The bell attached to the front door jingled. William entered carrying a white pastry box. He held it up. "Don't worry, Lily, this one contains nuts."

I laughed. "So, you heard about the boxes that were used from Sugar and Sprinkles."

His eyes grew serious. "I did. What a sad ending to a happy event."

My eyes caught sight of Gage and Nikki sauntering across the town square, headed in my direction. "I hope you have more than one cinnamon bun in there."

William turned to see them. "With you, I always know to include double what you order."

Gage pushed open the door, letting Nikki in before him, and said, "We're just in time for a coffee break."

He brushed his lips over my cheek, and that look he gave me caused my knees to quake like jelly. I kissed him back.

"William. Is there a chance you can work with Nikki on a special order?" I gave her a saucy wink.

Gage's face split into the widest smile. "Are you saying what I think you're saying?"

"As long as you agree."

Milo reached out and patted Gage's cheek. "Lily, does this mean you're about to request a wedding cake?"

I nodded. Tears welled up in my eyes. I wasn't sure why I was getting so emotional about a cake. "What do you think? Is it possible for you and Nikki to create a cake for our wedding? But you're sworn to secrecy since we're not ready to share the date, not quite yet."

Nikki threw her arms around Milo and me, and happy tears hovered on her lashes. William hugged Nikki and Milo and me, and then Gage wrapped his arms around us too.

Soon, we were all standing in the middle of my bookstore discussing cake flavors.

"My dear witch, does this mean I can have a smoked salmon cake? After all, I will be the third most important person at the ceremony."

"Oh, Milo. We'll figure out something."

Gage laughed. "Let me guess, that was about smoked salmon."

Milo tipped his head and looked at Gage. "See, he *does* speak familiar."

If you loved Cranberries & Criminals help other readers find this book: **Please leave a review now!**
Are you ready to read more from the Lily and the gang in Pembroke?
Keep reading for a sneak peek at
Broomsticks & Blossoms
A Book Store Cozy Mystery Series
Order Now
Or
Shop at Lucinda Race

Not ready to stop reading yet? If you sign up for my newsletter at www.lucindarace.com/newsletter you will receive an excerpt for Cookies & Capers, the introduction of when Lily met Milo right away as my thank-you gift for choosing to get my newsletter.

Cranberry Bake-off Recipes

Cranberry Sauce Muffins
From: Donna W

Preheat oven to 400F

Ingredients:

½ cup brown sugar

¼ cup white sugar

1 cup Whole berry cranberry sauce (canned) or homemade

¾ cup milk

¼ cup vegetable oil

1 egg

1 tsp vanilla extract

½ tsp salt

2 cups flour

1 tsp baking powder

Line a 12-cup muffin tin with paper baking cups. Spray the inside of the paper baking cups with non-stick cooking spray. (Note: I used foil-lined baking cups so no need for cooking spray.)

In a large mixing bowl, add brown sugar, white sugar, cranberry sauce, milk

Vegetable oil, egg, cinnamon, vanilla extract and salt. Mix until combined. (Note: I tried to use as much of the whole cranberries as possible with a bit of the jelly.)

Combine flour and baking powder, mix into wet ingredients until well combined.

Distribute the muffin batter between the 12 muffin cups. (Note: I had enough for 14 muffin cups).

Put the muffins in oven to bake for 25 minutes. (Check at 20 minutes)

Homemade Cranberry Sauce
From Cathy M.B.

1/3 cup of white sugar
   1/3 cup brown sugar
   1/4 cup Water
   13 ounces fresh cranberries
   2/3 cup fresh squeezed orange juice
   1/2 tsp fresh grated ginger
   1/4 tsp dried ginger (optional)
Zest from 1 orange
Zest from 1/2 a lemon

Combine water, orange and sugar in a saucepan. Cool on medium heat until the sugar is dissolved, stirring occasionally.

Add the orange zest, lemon zest, fresh ginger, dried ginger, and fresh cranberries. Bring back to a boil. Reduce to simmer. Stir occasionally and cook until the cranberries have burst. You can cook longer to thicken more. However, it will thicken as it sits.

Orange Cranberry Cake
From Vicky Boyd

1 ½ cups flour

2 teaspoons baking powder

¼ teaspoon salt

1 cup sour cream

1 cup sugar

3 eggs

zest of 1 orange

juice from one orange

½ cup softened butter

1 ½ cups fresh cranberries or if you prefer a sweeter cake used dried and sweetened cranberries

Icing:

1 cup powdered sugar

2-3 tablespoon milk OR orange juice

Preheat oven to 350 degrees. Spray bundt pan and sprinkle with 2 tablespoons of sugar on the bottom. Add ¼ cup cranberries to the pan and set aside.

Cream butter and sugar until a lemon color, 4-5 minutes. Add eggs one at a time and mix well.

Add orange juice and zest. Add the sour cream.

Sift together the flour, salt and baking powder and add to the wet mixture. Stir in remaining cranberries.

Bake for 50-55 minutes until tester comes out clean. Let cool in the pan for 5 minutes. Turn out cake to wire rack and cool. Mix glaze ingredients and drizzle over the top and sides of the cake.

Honorable Mention Sue White
Cranberry Sweet Rolls

Thank you to everyone for sending me your recipes. It was difficult to choose just a few to include but keep reading my newsletter where I'll be sharing the baked goods as I make them with, pictures too!

A COZY WITCH MYSTERY

Broomsticks & Blooms
A BOOK STORE COZY MYSTERY
Book Ten
LUCINDA RACE

Chapter 1

Lily

I clapped my hands and spun around in a circle. The hem of my dark purple cloak fanned out around my feet. Milo sat on the kitchen table grooming his whiskers and paused mid swipe. "My dear witch. Must you?"

I scooped him up and twirled him too. "It's the most exciting night ever."

"Put. Me. Down." His deep kitty grumble left no room for doubt he was not a happy familiar.

Clutching him to my chest I kissed the top of his head, the gray downy soft fur tickling my nose. "Ah choo."

"That's what you get for rough housing with me."

I held him out, body dangling in mid-air and stared into his green eyes. "You did that on purpose."

He glanced at the floor. "Put. Me. Down." This time he actually swiped at me. Granted his claws were in but he wasn't a happy camper today.

"Milo, what's the matter? Do you feel well?"

"Other than waiting for my supper, as usual, I'm fine.

But I don't know why you're so excited about the council meeting tonight."

"I have my permit filled out to request flying lessons." I pulled him back to my chest and hugged him tight. "I can't wait to be able to take you for a ride on my broom."

"Lily, that's not how broom riding works. There are rules you know."

"Rules, smules. If I want to take one of the greatest witches, who happens to be my familiar for a ride, who'll stop me."

He shook his head. "You might be morphing into an adequate witch, but you still need to follow the rules of the coven. I know Aunt Mimi is in charge but still don't make her look bad by your flagrant thumbing of rules."

Setting him down on the table I said, "We have time for a quick snack, but I don't want us to be late. Nikki's going to meet us there."

"Well that's good, your personal Watson can go over the rules with you."

I couldn't help but grin when Milo referred to my bestie as Watson. Ever since I discovered I was a witch, our little town has had more than its share of murders. Being a puzzle loving gal, I jumped in and helped to solve the crimes. Most of the time Nikki was by my side, she was my ride or die and happened to be an amazing kitchen witch.

"I know what you're thinking. Nikki's amazing but she's a stickler for coven rules."

I tipped my head. "How do you always seem to know what I'm thinking? Are you sure you aren't telepathic?"

"When it comes to you, my favorite witch, you're an open book." He glanced around. "Speaking of, where's your book?"

I groaned. "Why is it several times a week you bring up my family's book, Practical Beginnings?"

"You have so much more to read and it's my duty to make sure you fulfill your potential as a witch." He gave me a pointed look. "Did you leave it at the bookstore again?"

"No. It's in my office. Do I need it for tonight?"

"You shouldn't, but before we go you should read a page or two. It might give you," he paused as if weighing his next comment, "a boost."

"Is that literally or psychologically?"

He jumped to the floor and padded into the living room. "Call me when my snack's ready. Any fish will do for now."

"How gracious of you my dear familiar." I wanted to stamp my feet at his infuriating tactics to get me to do the required reading that I so often neglected. But it always had the desired effect, my curiosity went into overdrive. After all, in just under two hours I would hold in my hand a permit to fly a broom.

The kitchen door opened and my handsome fiancé, Detective Gage Erikson, came in. He took in my cloak from my toes to neck. "Stunning. The coven won't have any choice but to grant your application. You look every inch of the perfect witch." He kissed me and then twirled me around.

Laughter bubbled up as the yards of purple fabric wrapped around us both. "You should put me down."

He did with another light kiss. "I wanted to give you the feeling of flying."

"I always feel like I'm floating on air when I'm with you." I gave him one more kiss. "What are you doing tonight?"

"Hanging with Dad. Mom will be at the meeting with you. Since Dad and I share the same non-magical streak, it's just easier for us to hang out, watch baseball spring training on television, and have a beer."

"Guys night. I get it." I crossed to the pantry and pushed my clue board aside. I hadn't needed to use it in several months, well since a judge at the Cranberry Bake-off died last Thanksgiving. I took a can of salmon from the shelf, then peanut butter and a loaf of bread.

"How about a sandwich for dinner?" I held up the pantry items.

Gage chuckled. "Cooking will never be your thing my darling witch." He strode across the kitchen and opened the door before disappearing outside. When he came back, he held two bags that bore the logo, Clam Bake. "Dinner."

Milo stuck his head around the corner of the arch. "Did I hear Detective Cutie mention the D word? And more importantly did he get me something too?"

"Milo." The warning tone in my voice did nothing to quell his grumble.

"Lily. If you won't feed me, maybe your future husband will."

Gage grinned. "Let me guess, Milo's hoping there's something in one of these bags for him too?" He placed them on the kitchen table and patted his leg. "Come here, old man."

Milo obliged but glared at me. "Who's he calling old and whatever happened to respecting your elders? This is what happens when you take up with a non-magical person."

I let him drone on. It was easier than trying to reason with him. "Pay no attention to Milo's caterwauling, he's just a little hangry."

Gage opened the bag. "Then he gets his very special fish first. Broiled cod sans the butter and crumb topping."

Milo looked from me to Gage and rubbed his body against Gage's arm. "Now we're talking."

Turning his back on us he delicately devoured his fish before I had the opportunity to unpack our dinners. When he was done, smacked his mouth. "That was excellent. My compliments to my future witch in law."

"Huh, that's not the right saying."

He gave me a baleful look. "It's the best I could come up with, I'm in a fish coma." He jumped to the floor and slunk down the hall. I assumed to get a nap in before we had to leave for our coven meeting.

I unfastened the cloak and hung it next to the door. Underneath I wore jeans and a tee shirt. "Gage, do you think this is appropriate for my meeting?"

"I've seen Mom get ready for a coven meeting and she usually wears jeans too. I think it's more comfortable under her cape."

"If Glinda can do it, then so can I."

My gaze drifted to the mouthwatering soft yeast rolls and containers of chowder. Or maybe bisque. Either was fine and it was so much better than a peanut butter sandwich. "If I hadn't already said yes to marrying you, this would have put it over the edge." I blew him a kiss and quickly filled bowls with chowder, then I hovered my hand over the surface and closed my eyes. "Heat soup before I eat, and then I need to beat feet. For this I wish, so it shall be."

Gage laughed. "That's one of the most unusual spells I've heard you say yet."

I shrugged and flashed him a cheeky grin. "What can I say. I'm hungry."

"Then we should dig in. I wouldn't want you to faint away from starvation before you get that little slip of paper."

I waved the bowls to the table and his eyes widened. "Nice," was all he said before pulling out my chair and kissing my cheek. "You're very talented and I'm sure every witch in the coven recognizes you might be late to the caldron, but you've made up for lost time."

I beamed as he hugged me from above. "You say the nicest things to ease my nerves." I pressed my hand against my midsection and willed the gremlins to stop. I wouldn't call them butterflies since they'd been persistent all day and pushed me to the edge. "Thank you for all of this."

"You're welcome, Sweetheart."

Ninety minutes later Nikki and I were standing with Milo and her familiar, a golden retriever Murphy, in the thick of the woods away from the coven members who had gathered near the entrance waiting for the doors to open for the meeting.

"Are you ready," she asked.

"I've taken the preliminary test. All that's left is to have the council agree I'm ready to fly."

"You've memorized all the rules in case someone asks you a question?"

I shook my head no. "I didn't know there would be a pop quiz."

"It's not unheard of. They might go easy on you because of Mimi, or it could be just the opposite." She held up a small paperback book. "Rule number one, and the most important rule, until you pass the license test no other being can ride on your broom with you. After you have received it, double broom riding is permitted only with magical beings, such as your familiar or me."

"What about Gage or my mom?"

Her long strawberry blonde hair swung around her face,

and she shook her head. "Nope. That can lead to suspension of your license and possible revocation. Lily, don't think you can get around that one. The bottom line, witches have rules for a reason. We don't want non-magicals discovering our special skills. It might make things very difficult for us in Pembroke Cove."

"Don't they already suspect something? I mean, I've made things appear and disappear in the heat of a moment. Aunt Mimi provides healing remedies for witches and non-magicals alike. Don't they find that odd? And you're like a baker on steroids. Doesn't anyone wonder how you accomplish so much in such a short amount of time?"

"People will believe what they want. As for all of this," she waved her wand through the night air, "it's behind a shroud of magic. It can only be seen if you're intentionally looking for it." She nodded to the path. "Ready?"

Inhaling through my nose and a loud whoosh of an exhale followed, I squared my shoulders and stiffened my spine.

Nikki laughed. "You're not facing a firing squad."

She looped her arm through mine and pulled me down the path. I didn't need that much encouragement, but it was always nice to have her in my corner. "Hey, any chance on the way home we can swing by Blooms? I stopped by a couple of days ago and Madeline was busy. I think she was on the phone with a supplier, but she didn't look happy. When I went by today to talk about ideas for the wedding, the shop was closed up tight, but the open sign was still on the door. If I can't get in to talk with her, I'm going to run out to Wee Flower Farm. Dee Skorput should have ideas for the perfect flowers for a September wedding."

"Sure. Now, we need to enter the meeting without talking." She whispered, "The council likes that kind of thing."

I made a zipper motion over my lips and did the cross my heart sign over my cloak.

Stepping into the meeting space was like walking through a waterfall into an alternate universe. Each meeting had been a different experience but tonight was a full-scale business meeting. We took seats halfway down the main aisle. Rowan Riley moved down two seats giving us room to sit. I smiled at Aunt Mimi who sat in the center of the head table. She inclined her head in my direction and winked. I exhaled a sigh of relief. Everything was going to be just fine.

Aunt Mimi tapped the table with the tip of her wand. The sound amplified as if it was a judge's gavel. "Please come to order." She waited for the witches to stop chatting with their neighbors before continuing. "I will now bring this April meeting over the Pembroke Cove coven to order."

A smattering of applause followed her statement.

"First, we'll review old business and Glinda Erikson will read the report. Then my brother Reed Michaels, who has joined us tonight, will introduce new business. Then we will discuss the approval of a permit and license for witchy activities." She nodded to Glinda who smiled her thanks.

"Good evening coven members." She tapped her wand at the base of her throat and quickly rattled off a list of topics that were discussed at the last meeting. When she was done, she placed her wand on the table.

Mimi looked to her left. "Thank you Glinda. Excellent reporting as always." She turned to her right. "Reed, you have the floor."

He pushed back his chair, rose to his feet and licked his lips. "My wife Mindy and I would like to expand our tea business to offer coffee blends. As most of you know Mindy isn't a witch but she has a gift for creating special blends that are quite soothing to witches and non-magicals alike.

We plan to sell them at fairs and to businesses in town." He sat down and ran a shaky hand over his short graying hair. I knew that gesture well, he was a bundle of nerves.

"Does anyone object to Reed and Mindy expanding their business?" Aunt Mimi waited for several long minutes and then tapped her wand on the table. "Approved." She gestured for me to rise. "Now, on to permit approvals."

I glanced around the room and noticed how many witches attended tonight. I stepped forward, handed my application to Glinda and cleared my throat. "I'd like to apply for a permit to begin broom flying lessons, please."

To order click here:
Broomsticks & Blooms
A Book Store Cozy Mystery Series
Order Now
Or
Shop at Lucinda Race

A Free Story for You

Have you enjoyed Cranberries & Criminals? Not ready to stop reading yet? If you sign up for my newsletter at www.lucindarace.com/newsletter you will received Cookies & Capers which is the start of Lily and Milo's adventure as my thank-you gift for choosing to get my newsletter.

Cookies & Capers

I stood in front of the old wood and glass door as I pocketed the keys to the Cozy Nook Bookshop. Aunt Mimi had signed her bookstore over to me. She said it felt like giving me her baby. But I loved the shop as much as my aunt did. We had worked together for the last twelve years. After attending the University of Maine, I had a degree in history and education. I had always wanted to be a teacher, but jobs were scarce and after substituting for a few years, I moved back to my hometown of Pembroke, Maine, and Aunt Mimi hired me as soon as I unpacked my suitcase.

Spending time with my aunt, learning the business, had been the best experience. I offered to buy the shop when she wanted to retire, but she wouldn't hear of it. As long as she had free books for life, and her long-term boyfriend Nate, she said it was a fair deal. From my point of view, I had built-in backup for years to come.

Now that I was the bookshop owner, Aunt Mimi was no longer coming in every day which meant her cat, Phoenix, wasn't either and the space felt empty without a kitty lying in the window or skulking about as kitties do. I was off to the Pembroke Animal Palace to see if I could find a match.

It was a short walk in the bright noonday sun. The spring air from the ocean carried a tang of salt, but the breeze was refreshing. I waved to one of my best friends, Gage Erikson, as he drove past in his police-issued sedan. My heart fluttered in my chest.

He was a detective on the force. Not that we had much crime in our small seaside town. But one of these days I was going to get brave and tell him I had been carrying a torch for him since we were in ninth grade. What's the worst thing that could happen? We'd still be best friends, right?

I continued down the brick sidewalk, waving to William North from the Sweet Spot Bakery. He was sweeping the area around the small bistro tables in front of the bakery. William was wearing a large pristine white apron and a wide smile. A deep inhale confirmed my suspicion. He was baking cookies. My mouth watered. I did a half turn and went back to where he was finishing up. "Good morning, William." I bobbed my head in the shop's direction. "What is that tantalizing smell?"

He held open the brightly polished glass door. "One of your favorites, Lily. Chocolate chip and pecan cookies. Can I interest you in one before you continue on your mission?"

I gave him a side-look. "Mission?"

He chuckled. "Over the years my Lulu had said you

had two speeds, strolling and purposeful. Just now it was purposeful so hence you're on a mission."

"I'm going to the shelter, hoping to find a kitty. The shop is lonely now that Phoenix is home every day with Aunt Mimi, and I think a cat napping in the window adds an air of serenity to the place."

"Unless you're allergic."

He had a point, but I was not willing to be deterred. I smiled. "I'm always happy to deliver to a customer." I leaned over the glass bakery case, like a kid pressing her nose against the candy case. "You made sugar cookies too and frosted them?" I sighed. I was going to need to exercise more if he continued to bake all my favorites. He was smiling at me as I looked up. "Are the chocolate pecan ready?"

He wiggled his eyebrows. "I have a tray cooling in the back."

"Then can I have one of those and a sugar cookie, but to go?"

With a flick of his wrist, he snapped open a white bakery bag and called over his shoulder. "Jerilyn, would you please bring out the last batch of cookies?"

I heard a muffled, coming, and smiled. "It's good that Jerilyn stayed on." I said nothing about his beloved wife Lulu. Rumor had it she was ill and not doing well.

He nodded. "It is. She's a hard worker and excellent with the customers."

Jerilyn bustled in from the back room carrying a large stainless-steel tray. It was lined with parchment paper and cookies the size of the palm of my hand. It was going to taste so good with a hot cup of tea later.

William put two in the bag, along with two sugar cookies, and then he handed it to me. I paid for my cookies and thanked him. "Stop by the shop later. You might just get to meet my new fur baby."

"Sounds like a plan." He grinned and crossed his arms over his rounded midsection. "You're more like your aunt than you realize. Ever since she opened that bookshop, she's had a cat, too."

I paused, tucked the bakery bag in my tote, and with my hand on the door, I turned and gave him a wide grin. "And now it's time I carry on the tradition." With a jaunty wave, I called, "Wish me luck."

Cookies & Capers is only available by signing up for my newsletter – sign up for it here at <u>www.lucindarace.com/newsletter</u>

Love to Read?

**All ebooks and signed paperback copies can be ordered from my website at:
Shop at Lucinda Race**

Cozy Mystery Books
A Bookstore Cozy Mystery Series
<u>Books & Bribes</u>
It was an ordinary day until the book of Practical Magic conked Lily on the head causing her to see stars. And then she discovered her cat, Milo, could talk.

Catnaps & Crimes
The fun continues as Lily practices her magic and needs to investigate another murder.

Tea & Trouble
A fall festival, reading tea leaves and a few clues propel Lily into a new murder investigation.

Scares & Dares

Love to Read?

What goes wrong at a haunted house is anything but expected until Lily starts following the clues.

Holidays & Homicide
Can Lily solve a murder before it ruins the holidays?

Leprechauns & Larceny
Will a dead leprechaun take the shine off the wedding?

<u>Magicians & Murder</u>
When four magicians roll into town for a show more than fun is on one person's mind.

<u>Artifacts & Amulets</u>
Milo has been keeping secrets, which can be deadly.

<u>Cranberries & Criminals November 2024</u>
Whose half-baked idea was it for bookstore owner and witch Lily Michaels to enter an amateur baking contest in her small town of Pembroke Cove, Maine?

Broomsticks & Blooms March 2025
The time has come for Lily to learn to fly.

Fishing & Forgery May 2025
A simple Sunday fishing adventure with friends where Lily and her friends reel in the big one.

Wands & Weddings June 2025
Lily and Gage are ready to tie the knot. But what's up with the coven's council? Can Lily unravel this new mystery before she says, I do.

Love to Read?

**Witches of Robins Pointe
A Paranormal Cozy Mystery Series**
Inherited Magic & Murder April 2025
Touch of Magic August 2025
Waiting for Magic October 2025

**Ghostly Gowns Series
A Paranormal Ghost Cozy Mystery Series**
Ghost and Gowns July 2025
Buttons & Burglary September 2025
Ribbons & Robbery November 2025

Cowboys of River Junction
Second Chances in Montana
Twenty years later Renee and Hank are back where they fell in love but reality is like a spring frost and is a long-distance relationship their only option for their second chance?

<u>Stars Over Montana</u>
The cowboy broke her heart but he never stopped loving her. Now she's back ready to run her grandfather's ranch...

Hiding in Montana
Can love flourish while danger lurks in the shadows?

<u>Moonlight Over Montana</u>
From the smoldering ash, she realizes he's all the family she and her daughter need.

Jingle Bells in Montana December 2025

The Sandy Bay Series
<u>Sundaes on Sunday</u>

Love to Read?

A widowed school teacher and the airline pilot whose little girl is determined to bring her daddy and the lady from the ice cream shop together for a second chance at love.

Last Man Standing/Always a Bridesmaid
<u>Barrett</u>
Has the last man standing finally met his match?

<u>Marie</u>
Career-focused city girl discovers small town charm can lead to love.

Price Family Romance Series
<u>Breathe</u>
Her dream come true may be the end of his...
Crush
The first time they met was fleeting; the second time restarted her heart.
<u>Blush</u>
He's always loved her but he left and now he's back...the question, does she still love him?
<u>Vintage</u>
He's an unexpected distraction, she gets his engine running...
<u>Bouquet</u>
Sweet second chances for a widow and the handsome billionaire...

Holiday Romance
<u>The Sugar Plum Inn</u>
The chef and the restaurant critic are about to come face to face.
Last Chance Beach
<u>Shamrocks are a Girl's Best Friend</u>

Love to Read?

Will a bit of Irish luck and a matchmaking uncle give Kelly and Tric a chance to find love?

A Dickens Holiday Romance
<u>Holiday Heart Wishes</u>
Heartfelt wishes and holiday kisses...

<u>Holiday Heart Wishes</u>
Hockey, holidays, and a slap shot to the heart.

<u>Christmas in July</u>
She's the hometown girl with the hometown advantage. Right?

<u>A Secret Santa Christmas</u>
Christmas just isn't Holly's thing, but will a family secret help her find the true meaning of Christmas?

Holiday Romance Box Set
Sweet with a touch of heat holiday romance novels.

It's Just Coffee Series
<u>The Matchmaker and The Marine</u>
She vowed never to love again. His career in the Marines crushed his ability to love. Can undeniable chemistry and a leap of faith overcome their past?

The MacLellan Sisters Trilogy
<u>Old and New</u>
An enchanted heirloom wedding dress and a letter change three sisters lives forever as they fulfill their grandmothers last request try on the dress.
<u>Borrowed</u>

Love to Read?

He's just a borrowed boyfriend. He might also be her true love.
<u>Blue</u>
Will an enchanted wedding dress work its magic one more time?

McKenna Family Romance Series

<u>Lost and Found</u>
Love never ends... A widow who talks to her late husband and her handsome single neighbor who has secretly loved her for years.
<u>The Journey Home</u>
Where do you go to heal your heart? You make the journey home...
<u>The Last First Kiss</u>
When life handed Kate lemons, she baked.
<u>Ready to Soar</u>
Kate will fight for love, won't she?
<u>Love in the Looking Glass</u>
Will Ellie's first love be her last or will she become a ghost like her father?
<u>Magic in the Rain</u>
Dani's plan of hiding in plain sight may not have been the best idea.

After All These Years February 2025
Arielle Clark is a famous artist with a painful past. When her first love comes to town, ghosts from the past are resurrected. But can the embers of love still linger after all these years?

Social Media

Follow Me on Social Media

Like my Facebook page
Join Lucinda's Heart Racer's Reader Group on Facebook
Twitter @lucindarace
Instagram @lucindaraceauthor
BookBub
Goodreads
Pinterest

About the Author

Award-winning and best-selling author Lucinda Race is a avid fan of fiction. As a young girl, she spent hours reading cozy mystery and romance novels and getting lost in the fun and hope they represent. While her friends dreamed of becoming doctors and engineers, her dream was to become an expert at crafting a captivating novel.

As life twisted and turned, she found herself writing nonfiction but longed to turn to her true passion. After developing the storyline for the McKenna Family Romance series and the Paranormal Cozy Nook Bookstore Series, it was time to start living her dream. Her fingers practically fly over computer keys. She weaves paranormal cozy mystery stories and romance with guaranteed happily ever afters.

Lucinda lives with her two little dogs, a miniature long hair dachshund and a shitzu mix rescue, in the rolling hills of western Massachusetts. When she's not at her day job, she's immersed in her fictional worlds. And if she's not writing mystery, suspense or romance novels, she's reading everything she can get her hands on.

www.ingramcontent.com/pod-product-compliance
Lightning Source LLC
Chambersburg PA
CBHW061254210726

48293CB00003B/955